Billionaire Desires

Tammy Godfrey

Phoenix Voices Publishing

Copyright © 2023 by Tammy Godfrey

All rights reserved.

No part of this publication may be reproduced, stored or transmitted in any form or by any means, electronic, mechanical, photocopying, recording, scanning, or otherwise without written permission from the publisher. It is illegal to copy this book, post it to a website, or distribute it by any other means without permission.

This novel is entirely a work of fiction. The names, characters and incidents portrayed in it are the work of the author's imagination. Any resemblance to actual persons, living or dead, events or localities is entirely coincidental.

Tammy Godfey asserts the moral right to be identified as the author of this work.

Tammy Godfey has no responsibility for the persistence or accuracy of URLs for external or third-party Internet Websites referred to in this publication and does not guarantee that any content on such Websites is, or will remain, accurate or appropriate.

Designations used by companies to distinguish their products are often claimed as trademarks. All brand names and product names used in this book and on its cover are trade names, service marks, trademarks and registered trademarks of their respective owners. The publishers and the book are not associated with any product or vendor mentioned in this book. None of the companies referenced within the book have endorsed the book.

Contents

Dedication	1
Acknowledgement	2
1. Chapter One	3
2. Chapter Two	11
3. Chapter Three	22
4. Chapter Four	32
5. Chapter Five	43
6. Chapter Six	55
7. Chapter Seven	66
Welcome to The Jade's Inn Family Excerpt	67
Chapter One	84
Chapter Two	96
About the Author	114

Dedication

This book is dedicated to Dirk Godfrey. I love you, in a way that the heavens themselves will never understand.

Acknowledgement

To my editor and proofreader Dirk Godfrey, Angela Metzger and Alorah Neibaur, for making my novel better than I thought it could be.

Thanks to Dyana Delaney for giving me the name of this book and helping with other names. For always being there when I need someone to talk to and understanding that talking to someone is the best medicine of all. Thanks to my husband who has always been there for me. To my son, Kelton who just a great kid. To my mom and dad for their love and support, you are what makes life better. To Jamie Godfrey, I want to thank you for making me take breaks when I wanted them or not. You remind me every day that life is important and that your hugs bring joy to my life. To Gavin and Asher, my joy and bright star in everything you do. Sometimes the simplest things are the things that matter the most.

Chapter One

New Job

"Why does the boss want to see me?" I said aloud as Piper came up to me.

"Relax Avery," Piper said. "Everything will be fine. Just breathe and stop pacing a hole in the imported carpet." Avery sat, crossed her legs, uncrossed them and crossed them once again before standing as the door to the bosses' office swung open. The typical insincere laughter came out first, followed by Mr. Foster, AKA the boss. He was shaking hands and patting the back of some man in a suit that was about twenty years out of fashion. The man left, and Mr. Foster returned to his office.

"Avery, he's ready for you," Piper announced, opening Mr. Foster's door. Avery walked in with trepidation.

"Please sit Miss. Dodd," Mr. Foster said. "I've been watching you, and I like what I see. I notice you've applied for the executive assistant position and are more than qualified for it." Avery was flattered, but before she could respond, Mr. Foster continued.

"I know you know my son, Grayson. He has been assigned as CEO of the new marketing branch, but he's so busy that he can't seem to schedule his work so that he can make time for his family," Mr. Foster explained.

Avery was confused, "Mr. Foster, I don't see how I can help. Your son is dedicated to his work." she concluded as she bit her lower lip. *To be honest Grayson was a pain in the ass but he was great at his job,* Avery thought. *That's why he couldn't keep an assistant longer than a month. They would always quit. There were always bets going on in the break room of how long the latest assistant would last.*

Mr. Owen Foster saw the look of uneasiness and confusion flash across her face. Chuckling to himself, he could not wait until his son saw this young woman. *She's stunning, as well as strong*, Mr. Foster thought, eyeing her with keen interest. *A strong woman was exactly what Grayson needed. Avery had been working here for three years in other departments. When she thought something was wrong, she would voice her opinion even to me, the president of the company. Greyson is a little harder to talk with, let alone confront. This will be interesting.*

"Miss. Dodd, Avery, if I may, I want to promote you to the position of Executive Assistant to my son. This position will include a new title, your own office, and significance increase in salary," Owen explained.

It would have to be a very big salary increase to be willing work for his son, Avery thought to herself. With a promotion and salary increase, though, she could quit her night job and spend more time with Adam. That would be a great perk.

Owen allowed her some time to think about it, and a week later Avery accepted the position as Executive Assistant for Grayson Foster.

Avery was talking to Mr. Foster about accepting the job after a board meeting when his son walked in, "Son, I want you to meet your Executive Assistant, Miss. Avery Dodd."

Grayson turned, and before him stood a woman who was stunning. She was a few inches shorter than him, with lovely light skin that looked like it was kissed by the sun, blue-green eyes, caramel hair that was cut past her shoulders but styled into the latest fashion, and a body that was firm, as if she went running every day. Grayson's blood heated at the sight of her. He had seen her before and knew she was good at her job. She had even gone toe to toe with his dad and won the fight.

"Miss. Dodd, I don't know what my father promised you, but I can promise you, this will not be a fluff job," he said as he stood.

Avery straightened herself as tall as her five-foot-five-inch frame would allow her and looked Grayson in the eye. "Mr. Foster, I don't do fluff, and I look forward to working for you." Avery knew tomorrow was going to be a big day, so when she was dismissed for the day by her new boss, she gladly accepted. Her mind was filled with cardboard boxes packed full of office supplies, personal photos, plants, both plastic and real, and naked trolls with purple hair, all ready to move to the office of the new Executive Assistant to Grayson Foster tomorrow.

With excitement disguised as grace and tact, she left and walked with a purpose to the bus stop. Her excitement could not be contained. However, she took out her cell and began to yell into it, even as she approached the bus to take home.

"Honey, I got the job," Avery shouted with her outside voice as she dropped into the first available seat. "This job comes with a raise, and we can live easier now. I can even quit my night job so we can have more time together."

"I'm so excited for you," Adam, her boyfriend of five years said without sounding genuine. "Do you still want me to go back to my family business this fall? It's only for two months?"

"If you look for a job in town, I'm almost certain you'll get one. Then you won't have to go to the family farm in the fall," Avery said. "I think you should go back to school."

"I'll get the paperwork done and we will see," Adam said. "I still think I should go to the family farm, because you're going to be busy with your new job. On the plus side, now we can get that new place we've been looking at."

"This is the best day ever," Avery squealed, jumping up and down, to the dismay of the other passengers. "We should celebrate," Avery suggested. "I mean go out; you know to dinner. I'm not talking burgers or tacos. I mean a real dinner, with chairs and table clothes, and spoons and two forks, none of which we would have to wash."

"Okay, I get it," Adam laughed. "Fine dining, not fast food. Do you have a place in mind?"

Avery continued speaking at a high volume about various restaurants, covering the entire ethic gambit within their town, plus two towns over. The other passengers became hungry and helpful, shouting out suggestions. Avery settled on the new Indian place in old town. When Adam asked why, her answer was simple.

"Because we've never tried it," Avery was clearly the braver of the two, a fact that did not go unnoticed by Adam, even on their first date.

"There are other ways we can celebrate," Adam said suggestively.

Avery's outside voice suddenly became an inside whisper, "Yes, we can." She was grateful that the bus came to a stop not far from her home. Her pace quickened the closer she got to her front door, motivated by the goosebumps that Adam created by his amorous suggestion.

The door slammed with a resounding thud as they fell back against it. Adam's hands began to caress her shoulders. A light kiss along her jaw made her shudder. The anticipation of what might happen was driving her wild.

As their lips met, electricity shot through Avery's body. Adam's soft tongue parted her mouth and met hers. His palms slid down her shoulders and found her lower back. He pulled her tight against his chest. As their kiss deepened, she felt her knees grow weak. She walked backward toward the bedroom, and Adam followed. When her legs hit the edge of the bed, she knew where she wanted to be.

They sat down and resumed their passionate kissing. Adam's hand found its way to her hip and began to caress slowly down to her thigh. She trembled feeling his touch. She reached out and placed her hand on his chest. She felt his chiseled pecks beneath his light-weight shirt. Their lips separated and he looked into her eyes. Staring back at him, she nodded.

He slowly unbuttoned the top button of her blouse, then the next one. He reached the last button and parted the silk to each side. Avery's breast fit neatly into her lace bra. Her flat stomach was soft and pale. She stood up in front of him and shrugged the blouse from her shoulders, letting it fall to the floor. She grabbed the bottom of his T-shirt, and he lifted his arms over his head as she peeled the shirt from his hard body. He put his hands on her hips and slid her skirt down, revealing matching panties. She turned her back to him showing off her tight little butt. She reached between her shoulder blades and unclasped her bra. Letting the straps fall from her shoulders, the bra slipped to the floor. She turned back around, her arm and hand covering her tiny mounds.

He stood and stepped toward her, placing his palms on her slender hips, pulling her close. She put her arms around his neck and their chests pressed against one another. When their lips parted, her hands made their way down to his belt. She unclasped the belt and then unbuttoned his jeans. The zipper was next. She slowly slid the zipper down. She guided his jeans over his hips until they dropped. He stepped out of the fabric that had gathered at his feet. The two were now standing in nothing but their underwear. The ample bulge in his boxers made her body tingle. It had been a while since they had been together, and she was enjoying it. He quickly grabbed her by the hips and picked her up. She threw her legs around his waist. Her tiny nipples were pointing straight at his face. He took one in his mouth and sucked gently then slightly nibbled. She let out a gasp and moaned softly.

He turned and put her down on her back. The mattress accepted her gently. He brought one of his hands up to the other mound on her chest and lightly pinched the nipple. Her breast was enveloped in his palms as he gently squeezed. He grabbed the elastic band running around her waist. She lifted her hips as he slid the panties past her ass. He threw the small wad of lace on the floor and looked at the perfect body lying in front of him.

She nodded at him again. He stood up and pushed his boxer briefs to the floor. As he climbed onto the bed, she watched his member as it grew harder. He came to rest next to her on the bed.

He rolled toward the nightstand and reached into the drawer. His hand emerged with a small square package. He removed the condom and slid it down his member, climbed on top of her, and positioned himself between her legs. After one last silent conversation, he slid his member into her center. As he pushed further, a wince escaped her. He felt a pressure against the tip. He pushed through, and she let out a shout of pain that reminded her that Adam never made sure she was ready. After a moment, he pushed the rest of his member into the tight hole.

She whined.

She was tight as he slid in and out of her. He had never felt anything like it before. She whined louder, as he thrust in and out. It always hurt, and Adam never seem to care. He moved in and then out and then exploded. Three minutes-that was all the time it took. When his tremors subsided, he guided himself out of her.

She stood up, making her way to the dresser. She slid on a tee-shirt to cover herself.

"Was it good for you?" Adam asked. Avery knew how to answer that question, and it was not what she really wanted to say.

"Adam you were amazing," Avery gushed, but what she was thinking was she did not want to have another fight about sex. *I've tried to get him to be more creative in the bedroom. I thought he would think outside of the box when it came to sex, after all, he's an artist working with clay and so on. I always heard stories about artists being great in bed, but Adam just isn't.* As Adam went to go get 'cleaned up,' she went to the kitchen to make dinner. Her cooking time was always her thinking and de-stressing time.

We talked about doing oral sex one time, but after I went down on him, he said he hated it. What guys says they hate that? He's never gone down on me because he said the idea of it makes him sick. I wish he would try once or just play with me more, so it doesn't hurt as much, but he says he likes it better with I'm small. The trouble is it hurts like hell. I only hope that things change. I don't want to fight tonight, but I need to talk to him about it soon.

Five months later, Avery and Adam were in a new house. Adam had gone back to the family farm for planting and came back, but still didn't have a job or any plans for going back to school. Adam just sat around until harvest, once again leaving Avery home alone. Adam had originally gone to school to be an artist in sculpting, drawing, and painting, but after he had graduated, he did a couple of jobs and then quit, saying that his muse was not working.

Avery loved him and knew Adam would get a job soon. She had to pay all the bills, but she kept telling herself that when Adam got a job, she could relax. Until then, Avery would have to keep both Grayson and Adam happy.

When Grayson started asking her to work longer hours, she had done it. More money would make life easier; she had thought. But after a month of long nights and weekend meetings, Adam wanted her to stop, to cut back on the long nights and weekends because he missed her. When Avery asked him to get a job so she could work less, Adam only changed the subject. Avery had no choice but to continue working as many hours as Grayson wanted until Adam decided to get a job.

Chapter Two

A Year Later

One word could describe her boss, Grayson Foster: sexy. An attractive man from heaven above, most women would say. He was six-foot-one-inch tall. He had deep olive skin, hair the color of chocolate that was cut short to his head, and the most fascinating brown eyes. He embodied sex by the way he walked and talked, but he seemed to have no interest in it; work was always on his mind.

However, even though he was an extremely handsome man, no one liked him. He was rude and blunt with people. The only people who ever tried to interact with him at all were his parents, immediate family, a couple of friends, and his cousin from across the country, Cole. Then there was Penelope. All that can be said about her is that she was from a very rich family, and she had her eyes set on Grayson since the first day she started working for him.

Penelope thought everyone was below her, including Avery. The way she walked into Grayson's office uninvited got Avery in trouble every time Penelope came over to see him. She had blond hair that was as long as Avery's, but it shined like someone brushed it a hundred times every day. Maybe she had a hair stylist at her house each morning just to make the blond look gold. Penelope was a size zero body, no fat anywhere. She looked like a runway model. She always wore red fingernail polish. Penelope was maybe an inch shorter than Grayson, and together they would make a great cover for a romance book. There was one thing Avery always thought was wrong with Penelope, and that was her nose. She had the nose of a snob, but when you saw her, it fit her.

When Penelope wanted to have Grayson go to dinner with her, she would ask Avery if he had time. The standing order from Grayson was that he never had time for dinner, unless it was a party he had to go to, and then Avery always had to plan it—generally, in advance.

Grayson did not want anyone interfering in his life. Avery planned trips for him and made purchases he didn't have time for, like sending out gifts for birthdays or the holidays. She even tried to set up time for him to visit his family, which he would do only if she was with him.

When Avery had joked about getting a buzzer for her desk that would lock his door so he wouldn't be interrupted, he had her call the lock smith to see if it was possible. It was, so Grayson had it done. When his father asked him about it, he had said it was Avery's idea.

The first time Avery used it on Penelope, you would have thought someone had killed her. She screamed, making Mr. Foster come to see what was going on. This gave Grayson enough time to leave through the back door of his office, but it pissed off Penelope to no end. It ended up making her more difficult to deal with for both Grayson and Avery.

Whenever he traveled, Avery accompanied him on trips. She was a steady date when he needed a companion for social functions, and this made Penelope mad to say the least. In addition, Avery had to always be available if he needed her to come in.

She was also very pretty, and for him, that was distracting. So, he did everything he could to make her quit. He disapproved of her style of dress, her lifestyle, and even refused to greet her when he arrived at work. She didn't know why she put up with his crap; none of the other assistants had to deal with stuff like this from their bosses. Avery was aware of a number of people who wanted to hire her to be their assistant. She kept a list in the back of her mind, and some days she checked it twice. He implemented a strict dress code for all of his employees. At no time was casual wear allowed. This was a business, and only professional wear was accepted.

Every morning, Avery felt like she was being inspected when entering his office. He would make her stand up, he would walk around her, and then either say nothing and sit down, or tell her she had to change into something more professional. Then Avery would give him the itinerary for the day. Since working for him, she had to be on time and meet all of his specifications.

This weekend, however, Avery had plans. She and her boyfriend were planning a getaway. This was their last-ditch effort to try and save their relationship. With her working all the time, and Adam staying home all day long, Avery didn't know what to do. Adam worked a total of five months a year. This earned about a quarter of what she made, and it was always used on a small project, like getting the car fixed or buying the latest video game system. This meant she had to work at least 60 hours a week so she could pay all the bills.

"Miss. Dodd, we will leave for Houston early. Make sure you are ready on time. I don't want to have to wait on you like the last time," Grayson Foster informed her once he called her in to debrief at the end of her workday.

Avery was confused. "Wait, Mr. Foster, I requested time off this week, and it was approved. Ms. Williams will be accompanying you to Texas this week," She explained. "I even had her take the dance classes so you would have a dance partner."

"No, I had them deny your request and you will be accompanying me. Cancel your plans with your boyfriend; you're busy," Grayson didn't even bother looking up from his itinerary as he delivered the news.

Avery was ticked. She had put in her request over two weeks ago and received her confirmation email just last week. "They approved my days off. I have an email to prove it," Avery told her boss who seemed to become happier by the minute. "Miss. Dodd, you might want to check your email again," Grayson informed her smugly.

She felt her anger build and knew there wasn't anything she could do but say, "Yes, sir."

Grayson looked in her eyes and he could see her fury. He loved the way her blue-green eyes turned darker when she became upset. However, she was a consummate professional and he knew she would never argue with a superior at the job.

He suspected that under her calm exterior beat the heart of a woman full of passion and vigor, and at this moment, anger.

"Excuse me," Avery stood to go check her email. Sure enough, she had been sent a message denying her request for time off. The supposed consolation was that they gave her time off for next weekend instead of this weekend.

"Damn it!" Avery shouted, much to Grayson's amusement.

Avery took a deep breath. She had to calm down and keep her temper in check. She didn't need to lose her job, but she needed this weekend. She had already made plans and Adam had given her an ultimatum. If she canceled for any reason, this time he was leaving for good.

Making her way into Grayson's office, she tried to reason with him. "Mr. Foster, I know that this trip is important for you, but is there any way you can have Ms. Smith or even Ms. Williams to accompany you? I really need this week for personal reasons," Avery begged to her boss.

"Hmm," he pretended to think about it for half of as second. "Nope. My father, in his wisdom, selected you to assist me, and you accepted the job. Now I have to travel and need your assistance. So, Miss. Dodd, be ready in the morning. I will pick you up at seven."

Avery turned in a huff, muttering every expletive that popped in her head. She rushed to her car, and once the door was closed, she let loose a verbal tirade that lasted until she pulled into her driveway. Adam rushed to meet her, but the look on her face must have said everything because he stopped short.

"No! No Avery, you promised! You promised me this weekend!" Adam screamed as he became agitated and shoved Avery away from him.

"Adam, I'm sorry. He had my leave denied. There is nothing I can do," Moving to gather Adam in her arms, Avery tried to comfort her boyfriend.

Adam moved away. "You could quit. You don't have to work for him, you know. There are so many other places that would hire you. But you like him, don't you? He wants you; you know," Adam's voice matched his cold stare.

Throwing her arms up in frustration, Avery scoffed, "Adam, don't start this shit again. I love you. There's no one else. He's not attracted to me, he has Penelope. Listen, I'm sure-"

"I'm leaving, Avery. I can't do this anymore. He wants you and you want him. I'm just a third wheel," Adam stated. "I can't compete with him anymore. I'm moving this weekend."

Avery's short fuse blew, "You always do this. You know why I took this job. I was trying to be here for you. I was trying to make our lives better. If I didn't have this job, we'd still be living in that dump we were in two years ago."

Adam shook his head and stared at Avery for a moment. "You're too blind to see the bright light blaring in your face. Avery, I'm out."

Avery didn't know what to make of this. Adam always threatened to leave, but they were always threats. "Adam if you would just get a job in town, I wouldn't have to work all these hours," she tried explaining patiently.

"That's not the reason you are working so much," Adam said.

"Wait, what do you mean? What are you talking about, Adam? Let's talk about this when I get back. Please," she pleaded.

Without looking at her, Adam rose, walked to their bedroom, and retrieved his luggage. Taking out his phone, he made a call. "Hey, honey. Come get me. It's over with her," Pausing he nodded as the mystery person spoke. "I'll be waiting at the door. Love you too, bye."

Avery's head reeled. Adam was carrying three bags, and they were only supposed to be going to be away for the weekend. Also, who was this person, he was talking to? "Adam, what's going on?" she asked as her heart stopped.

Adam looked at her with an empty, distant glare on his face, as if they didn't know each other at all. "Well, you're not the only one who had someone on the side."

"Wait, wait, what do you mean? Adam, are you seeing someone else?" Avery asked shaking with a mixture of fury and pain. "Who, Adam? How long?"

"Really, you're demanding answers from me? You have been with him every night for over a year. You jump when he calls, run when he commands, hell, he even has you dressing like his personal sex kitten," Adam vented. "If you haven't fucked him yet, you will this weekend. He's groomed you to be the perfect woman for him, even I can see that."

"Adam, you're wrong. God! He's a workaholic. He doesn't even notice me!" Avery tried to explain. "Then there is Penelope, his girlfriend," she knew that was technically a lie, but she needed something. Honestly, she really didn't know what their relationship was.

Scoffing, Adam looked at her. "Oh really? When did you start wearing only skirts, thongs, and padded bras with fitted tops? You make yourself perfect every morning, when before you hardly wore any make up. You requested this weekend off four weeks ago, and yet, he declined it. Did you mention to anyone that we had plans?" Adam paused and waited for an answer.

Avery swallowed, "I mentioned we had a getaway planned to Mrs. Parks, his father's secretary, but she would not…"

"Were you in the office? Was he near?" Adam continued as he waited for his ride.

"Adam, come on, what does that have to do with anything?" Avery asked, while she thought about his question. *What is he talking about? Mr. Foster may have heard, but so what?*

HONK! HONK! A car horn blared from the driveway. Snapped out of her thoughts, Avery realized what was happening. "Adam, please. Don't leave," she begged.

Avery stood in front of Adam to prevent him from leaving.

Soon someone was banging on the door.

"Adam, are you ready, come on!" the woman yelled.

"I'm coming honey. Give me a minute," Adam yelled past Avery's head, then looked at her and shook his head in disappointment. "Bye Avery," he gently kissed her on the forehead and pushed her aside.

Adam walked to the door and let his new girlfriend in. "No, no! I won't let you leave me. You can't. I've done everything for you Adam," Avery sobbed.

"Hey, don't do this. Let him go. Don't do this," Adam's new lover whispered as she securely wrapped her arms around Adam; the two watched for a second as Avery fell apart. Finally, they left her to her pain and anger.

Avery, feeling broken and still trying to understand what just happened, went to her room, pulled out her suitcase and packed for her business trip. Then she showered and went to bed, hoping this was one of Adam tricks to make her do what he wanted when she gets back. It wouldn't be the first time he did this to her. The only difference is this time he brought in another girl to make his point.

When I get home from the trip, he will be here, she thought as she lay in bed, trying to fall asleep. She knew he would say he'd leave for good if she didn't give him more time.

Avery thought about her five-year relationship with Adam. For years, they had lived in cheap, dingy, and small efficiency apartments until her promotion over a year ago.

With her increase in salary, she bought them a nice threebedroom house. It wasn't perfect, but it was theirs. Adam seemed thrilled at first, but then Grayson started interfering with Avery's home life, and demanding more time helping with his new house. He wanted her to help buy furniture, have the painters come in, decorating, and so on to get the house ready so Grayson could move in. This was what had her working longer hours. She didn't want to do it, but Grayson had offered a bonus that would pay off all her student loans and she wouldn't have to work the long hours like before. Avery had explained this all to Adam. Adam had been happy at first, but now, not so much.

Grayson showed up the next morning and Avery did as she always did. She was a complete professional about everything. The business trip accomplished everything, and more than Grayson and Mr. Foster had hoped for. Avery called Adam many times, but he never called back.

Adam had done this before when they fought before a trip. The problem was, she just didn't feel the same about any of it this time.

* * *

Grayson knew Adam had cheated on Avery. He'd actually hired someone to follow him and take pictures of him cheating. He had planned to give them to Avery during this trip but had changed his mind when he saw she was not acting like herself.

When he first started to have feelings for this woman, he didn't know. They just kind of snuck up on him. He asked her to stay late one night for a marketing meeting, and then he had asked her to help him with his new house. He had offered her a good amount of money, because Avery had good taste and he didn't want Penelope getting her hands on it.

Do you know how hard it is to find a trusting person to help you? He realized he cared for her one day when he had asked her to stay late. A client had changed his mind, which meant they had to pull an all-niter to get a new concept before the meeting the next day. When Avery had come back from calling her boyfriend, she was crying. He didn't know what was said, all he knew was that the bastard made her cry, and that pissed him off.

It was right then that he decided to take her for himself. So, he had her work long hours and made her stay late. He called her on weekends, under the pretense of work, just because he wanted to be with her. Last week, when he heard her talking to Mrs. Smith about a weekend away with Adam, he had to stop it. One call to payroll ended those plans.

He knew they had fought, and he knew it was because he took back her weekend off, but he didn't know if the fight had been a really bad fight or a little one. Avery was very quiet. She did her job well, as always, but this time she seemed off. She didn't go off with some of the other people for drinks, like normal. She said she wasn't feeling well instead and went to her room. The plane ride home was even weirder. As they got closer to home, she got more and more quiet. When he dropped her off at her house, he knew they had gotten into a big fight. He felt bad leaving her there, after she sat in the car for a good five minutes before she got out.

* * *

Avery didn't know what to expect as she got out of the car. Was Adam's little trick real or not? As she walked up to the door, she heard movement and there was a strange car across the street from her house.

When she walked in, she didn't expect to see the slut sitting on her couch, boxes stacked everywhere, and a mess that would take hours to clean up.

"What is going on?" she yelled out. Adam came down from upstairs with a box full of stuff.

"I told you I'm moving out," Adam said. "I think I have everything. I took half of the food and all the DVDs, because I'm letting you keep most of the furniture."

"That hardly seems fair, since I paid for all the furniture and all the food and all the DVDs," Avery said.

"Baby, can you take this to the car so I can talk to her about getting my money back?" Adam asked, ignoring her argument. The girl grabbed the box, kissed him fully on the mouth, and then walked out.

"What money?" Avery asked.

"The money that I gave you a month ago," Adam said. "I want it back."

"That was the money for your new Xbox and games that you absolutely had to have three months ago," Avery was starting to raise her voice, anger overpowering her pain. "I'm not giving it back."

"Yes, you are," Adam said, "or I'll go to your job and tell your boss how much you love him and want to be with him. I'll make your life so bad there, that they will fire you."

Avery grabbed her purse, took out her checkbook, and wrote out a check for the money he wanted. She handed the check over. Adam folded it and put it in his back pocket. He started heading towards the door, then turned, "One more thing, your mother called, and I told her you were sleeping with your boss.

She's siding with me in all of this."

Avery snapped, "Get out! Get out of my house, Adam! I hate you! I hope you two rot in Hell," Avery yelled as she threw a lamp, books, and anything else she could reach. "GET OUT!"

Adam walked out, leaving Avery sobbing and broken in the living room of her empty home.

This was his fault; she knew that. She was so angry and disgusted with him that she didn't even want to think about him, but it was all Grayson's fault. He seemed to live to mess up her life. She never had a weekend off. He'd call with ridiculous requests at all times of the night. He acted as if he had the right to simply control her life.

She'd begged him to let her have this weekend, and he refused. It's not like he had a real reason to refuse, he just did it because he could.

She hated him. This was his fault, and he wouldn't even care that he'd destroyed the only thing that mattered to her.

Avery sat and cried all night. Down and crushed in spirit, she resolved that she would find a way to move on without Adam.

Chapter Three

After the Breakup

When Monday morning came, Avery had spent all night trying to get the mess that Adam had left cleaned up. She crawled into bed at five in the morning. Before she knew it, her alarm was sounding. It was time to dress for ass-wipe and go to work.

She was in the office half-an-hour early and ready to get through this day. All Avery wanted to do was go back to sleep. She had made an appointment with the HR about her vacation time being withdrawn. This was not the first time Grayson had done this, and she had to put a stop to it.

Avery had also made an appointment with Mr. Foster to ask for a transfer or a reference to start looking for a new job away from Grayson, but she knew she couldn't leave him till the house was done. The money from that would change everything in her life.

She walked into Grayson's office, dropped his planner and without saying a word, turned and walked out. Avery heard Grayson say her name, but she acted like she didn't hear him.

Her plan was to walk straight to the HR office when she heard Mr. Foster call her name. "Avery, what did Grayson do now?"

"I canceled her vacation time, so she had to go on the business meeting with me," Grayson said.

"Son, our employees have to take so much vacation time, or the company will have to answer to it," Mr. Foster said. "Avery, can we talk about this in the office, instead of HR getting involved, please?"

"Sir, no disrespect, but I really wanted this time off and this is the third time he's done this," Avery said. "I had plans for someone else to go with him. I did everything I could to make this business trip easy for him, but he still canceled my vacation again. I had asked for this leave four weeks ago. Sir, I did everything to not cause trouble and still..."

"Avery, go to my office please," Mr. Foster said. Avery turned to go to his office but all she wanted to do was file a report with HR.

"Dad, Avery is my employee, I will handle this," Grayson stated.

"Not this time son. This is the third time you have done this to Avery. She is a great employee, and you treat her like a slave," Grayson's dad said. "How about if I give you Penelope for a while, that way you can see and hopefully appreciate how much Avery does for you."

"No way in hell," Grayson blurted out. "I understand how good Avery is and I don't want anyone else."

"Then why do you treat her so badly?" asked, interested with the response. "Son, messing with her vacation time is wrong.

Reward the people who work well. Don't treat them badly."

"Dad, the problem is Kyle Anderson," Grayson began to explain. "He called me three days before our scheduled meeting to inform me that not only would he be there, but so would his daughter Lisa. He's trying to hook me up with his daughter. It's bad enough Penelope throws her man-hook me every time we pass each other here at the office, I don't need wanna-befather-in-law's parading their daughters around on the road. Avery is the only one who can keep these crazy fathers at bay. I told her she could have this weekend off."

"When did you tell her she couldn't take the time off?" Grayson's dad asked.

"Friday," Grayson replied.

"Morning or right before she was leaving for the day?" he asked knowing the answer.

"After I had her vacation time disapproved," Grayson said, avoiding answering the question directly.

"That's going to cost you son," Mr. Foster said and walked into his office.

"Sir, I know you gave me a raise to work with your son. I want to thank you for that, but I can't let him treat me like this anymore," Avery stated.

"I talked to my son, and I think I understand what's been happening," Mr. Foster said. "I have two ways to reprimanded him."

"Sir, I don't want him reprimanded. I want to be transferred somewhere else in the company," Avery said. "Your son needs a man to be his assistant, someone who can handle his special needs."

"What special needs?" Mr. Foster asked coming around his desk to sit. He knew this was going to be interesting. "Have a sit please Avery."

Avery sat and then stood up and started pacing again. Mr. Foster just watched her and waited for her to begin.

"Sir, your son is very dedicated to his job, and he is very blunt on what he wants. I think a male assistant would be better in the office, and a female assistant, or a very good-looking girl to go with him on his business meetings and family functions," Avery began. "Your son loves to dance and a girl on business trips would help."

"Do you dance with my son?" Mr. Foster asked.

"Yes, he keeps me on the floor after business dinners so the daughters that are invited to the dinner leave him alone. He dances with them a couple of times, then I'm the stand in for the rest of the night," Avery stated. "Maybe Penelope would be a good choice. She could handle the daughters and she knows how to act around the other businesspeople where I have trouble."

"What type of trouble?" Mr. Foster asked. This was interesting to say the least. He was having a hard time imagining his son dancing all night with Avery.

"I get a little upset with the girls always wanting his attention," Avery continued. "I mean, he's cute and all, but I want to strangle him at times. Then always having to dress perfect. I know I have to be professional, but I just don't measure up to the girls that come to these meetings. I think Penelope would be great for him," Avery picked up a pencil from the desk and started playing with it.

"Didn't you install a button to stop her just walking into his office all the time," Mr. Foster said.

"Yes, but that because he has to be sleeping with her or something. He's always hiding from her," Avery said.

Mr. Foster started thinking he missed something with his son. *Had he slept with Penelope? No, he wouldn't sleep with her, but I think he likes Avery. Well let's see what happens next.* "Avery this is what I was thinking, I can give you the week off to get a break from my son. Paid leave."

"I really think that you should start looking for a new assistant for him," Avery said. "My boyfriend left me because I'm working so many hours, and I feel that I could not be professional around him anymore. I really want to tell him off."

"I'm sorry about your boyfriend," Mr. Foster said, honestly meaning it. "Do you think talking to him will get him back?"

Avery stood up, walked around again, sat back down, then stood up again while she thought. *Adam cheated on me. There is no way in hell I was taking him back. It's not Grayson's fault for the breakup, not really. Adam didn't want to work. He wanted someone to take care of*

him. I was working long hours, but that was because he wouldn't work.
"I won't be getting back together with my boyfriend. It's over."

Right then Mr. Peterson, CEO in Manufacturing, came into the office, "Sir, I'm not taking Penelope on my business trip. I need someone who knows what they're doing."

"How about Avery here, could she help you with this business trip?" Mr. Foster offered. "Avery needs a break from my son, and I think you need a break from Penelope."

"Can't we just switch them permanently? Me have Avery and Grayson can have Penelope. She's always in his office driving Avery crazy, instead of doing her job for me anyway," Mr. Peterson said.

"I have one big project I'm doing for Mr. Foster, and I'll need a week to get it done," Avery said. "I can help Mr. Peterson with his business trip, if your son doesn't have a problem with it."

"Grayson will have a problem with it," Mr. Foster said with certainty, "but I think this will be good for him and the company. And I have seniority. If I tell him it's happening, it's happening."

"I can't take Penelope to this business meeting in Boston," Mr. Peterson said. "She has everything but the meeting on her brain." Avery started thinking that Penelope wasn't as great of an employee as she made herself out to be.

"Matt, have Penelope give everything on this business trip to Avery," Mr. Foster said. "Avery, I want you to give Penelope everything you're working on or meeting for the time you will be gone. Tell my son to come into the office. I'll explain everything."

"Yes sir," Avery said.

"Do you want me to break the news to Penelope or do you?" Mr. Foster asked Mr. Peterson. "Never mind, just tell her I want to see her too. Penelope needs her last warning, and I think my son might be the one to get her to quit." Avery smiled at that comment.

"Avery, we are leaving tomorrow morning, but I have a lot of things for you to get done before that," Mr. Peterson began.

"Can you be in my office in an hour after talking to Grayson? I'm sorry in advance, but it might be a late night."

"That's fine, it's not like I have anyone to go home to," Avery said, before thinking about it. She rose to her feet and made her way to Grayson's door. Her first knock was timid. Her second was not.

"Come in," Grayson said.

"Your father would like to speak to you," Avery said.

"We have pictures at one, so you need to go home and change into something more professional." Grayson said. "I'll pay to have your hair done; in fact, we can go to lunch after to celebrate." *The photo shoot, I forgot about it. That's why the morning was so free. Well, I guess Penelope can be in it instead of me. She'll absolutely love that.*

"Sir, I really think you need to talk to Mr. Foster before you send me home," Avery said. Grayson got up and headed out the door. She proceeded cautiously back to her desk and made a copy of all of Grayson's meetings for the week, including dinner meetings and so on. He did have a busy week. Perhaps Penelope could handle all this better, she thought. Maybe we could just change CEO's.

Avery began tapping all the familiar keys on her keyboard and started printing everything she thought she would need for the trip, and a few things she wouldn't. She included a few things for next week, just in case they didn't return as soon as they planned. She put everything in its proper folder, as usual, but had to catch her herself as she was walking toward Grayson's office. Instead, she turned and sought out Penelope's desk. She placed the folder on her desk, then walked away quickly, thumbing through her iPad to check her schedule and notes. She didn't want to miss a thing before morning. Avery was so tired from cleaning all night, and she still wasn't done;

that was all in addition to the plane flight, and the meetings she had gone to over the weekend. Maybe a lunch nap might help. She didn't want to, but she knew she needed to make a doctor appointment. There was no telling who else Adam had been dipping his wick into and what he had caught.

Avery tip-toed to Mr. Peterson's door and knocked. The door opened on its own. Inside, she found what she could only describe as the aftermath of a post-apocalyptic hurricane.

"What happened?" Avery asked.

"Penelope's idea of getting things ready for the trip," Mr. Peterson replied in a huff. "Please call me Matt. We will be working together this week, and I really don't want to be thinking of my father the whole time."

"Matt, let's start with the accounting figures, where are they?" Avery asked.

"Somewhere in this mess; I had them on my desk last night, and when I came in today this was what I found. Penelope came in early to help get stuff ready and then…this," Matt stated, spreading his arms to show her the mess. "It's like she's trying to get me fired."

"Well let's get it cleaned up," Avery suggested. She and Matt were on the floor going over all the papers like a jigsaw puzzle, trying to understand what went where when Grayson came through the door.

"What the hell? Avery, I want you back to work now," Grayson insisted.

"I am working; for this week I've been told I'm working for Mr. Peterson, and I come back to you next week," Avery told him.

"Mr. Foster said I get to use her this week to help with the problems Penelope caused, also since Avery and you are having problems," Mr. Peterson continued talking. "Mr. Foster said you needed a break from each other."

"We have the photo shoot today," Grayson said. "You're in it."

"The shoot is about you, not me," Avery began. "They don't need me, and if they want someone hot Penelope will be a better choice."

"Avery is right, I am a better choice for a photo shoot," Penelope said making her usual dramatic entrance. "Where is the folder for Grayson?"

Avery stood, left the office, and returned with the folder she had left on Penelope's desk. "Here it is," she said. "When I get Mr. Peterson's folder for the business meeting and trip, then I'll give you what I have."

"It's not ready yet," Penelope said. "Since we changed jobs, that means you have to do it now."

"Sir, I think this would be better in your hands than hers," Avery said. "From what I've seen in the last hour, Penelope can't be trusted." Avery handed over the file to Mr. Foster and he took it. "This is only for a week, but right now I have a lot of work to do."

"You're a bitch," Penelope said with a total disregard for office etiquette.

"Perhaps, but in a week, Mr. Foster will be missing me, and Mr. Peterson will be expecting more from you." Avery said.

Last minute scrambling was nothing new for Avery, and she has learned to expect the unexpected. Given that, Penelope is a bitch, a fuck-up, and pisses Avery off to no end. After coming up with a sexy southern accent for the benefit of the guy at the airline, Avery was able to secure the two tickets that Penelope forgot to buy. After a few hours of scrambling to get things caught up, she made a beeline to her office where she knew her Papa Smurf stress ball was waiting to be squeezed. Once she arrived, her attention was diverted by Grayson's office door being open. Grayson did not like his door being left open. She peeked inside, afraid of what she would find, but she found nothing. The office was empty. She always loved the couch in Grayson's office, and when she sat down, it was only supposed to be for a moment.

* * *

Who left my door open? Grayson thought as he went to his office. Penelope is a piece of work. If there is anything missing... then he saw her, asleep and beautiful. At first, he just watched, then he walked over to his couch. He bent over and kissed her forehead. "Honey, time to wake up sweetie," Grayson said in a whisper.

He smiled, knowing she would never know he kissed her.

"Grayson, why are you so mean to me?" Avery said with her eyes closed.

Was she sleeping? "I like you," he said, very close to her ear, hoping she was still asleep. The loud voice that followed ensured she was awake.

"Grayson is mine for a day, and I find you going at it in his office?!" Penelope bellowed. Avery shot up and rolled into Grayson. She jumped a second time, blushing when she realized whose arms, she was in.

"We are not going at it," Grayson said. "And you will not call me by my first name, ever."

"But it's after working hours," Penelope said in a more pleasant, but whiny voice.

"Avery was fixing your mess all day today and came to see me to make sure she had everything done before she left. I wasn't here, and she fell asleep on my couch because she had a long weekend working for me," Grayson started. "If Avery wants to see me or call me for any reason, you are to send it though. Do you understand?"

"Yes Gray...sir," Penelope said.

"Avery you better get home, Adam's going to be missing you," Grayson said. "You have my private number; call me if you need me."

"Adam is not an issue," Avery whispered, not knowing Grayson could hear her as she left the office to return home and pack. She needed to focus. If she did everything right, she would get five hours of sleep before Mr. Peterson is come to pick her up in the morning.

Chapter Four

Two Months Later

It had been six weeks since the business trip had come and gone. Pie charts were printed and filed, efficiency reports exaggerated, and a production meeting canceled and rescheduled. Office life had gone back to normal once Avery returned to work as Grayson's assistant. But, it wasn't the same normal—it wasn't like before.

Once Grayson had been fully exposed to the back-ass ward circus that was Penelope, he seemed calmer, even pleasant at times, and much more appreciative of Avery. As for Penelope, she quit after the realization that Grayson wanted nothing from her except hard work. There had been a party that began about 2.5 seconds after Penelope's car made its final left turn out of the parking lot. Someone had even brought cake.

Avery was sorting through the office mail for the day, mostly the same old junk, but she stopped when she came across the magazine. The pictures that she and Grayson and Penelope posed for were in this magazine. Grayson and Penelope's picture was on the cover. She was wrapped around him like a lover, her red fingernails highlighted against his black suit.

Avery found the article and began to read, and the more she read, the angrier she got. When she was done, she had homicide in her heart and an iPad in her hands. She had to know if the article was online yet. Sure enough, it was online too. Fuck.

In a world of business, timing is everything, and Grayson's timing, which has always been impeccable, was off when he walked into the office just in time to see an iPad flying over his head.

"You approved that article?" Avery screamed. "I have been your assistant for two years. I worked my ass off, and now everyone who reads this trash will think that bitch did all the work, while I was just another co-worker that was difficult to work with."

Before Grayson could say a word, Avery took the magazine, which was now just a crumpled wad of paper, and threw it at her boss. "I'm going home for the rest of the day, which according to the article, I do all the time. This next business trip will be our last. When we return, I will be speaking with your father. I will give him two choices; he finds me a new boss, or I quit," Avery stormed out.

Grayson retrieved the crumpled magazine and began to read the article just as his father came into the room, with a look of bewilderment on his face. "Grayson, what did you do now?"

"Fuck, fuck, fuck," Grayson said. "Father, I didn't approve this article. I would have never approved this article." Grayson was still reading, but his father took it from him to see what was going on.

"This is not the picture you had picked," his father said. "Who did you send it to? I need to know who to talk to."

"I fixed the article. This was one of the three covers they sent, but I didn't think it looked professional, so I went with one of just me. The article talked about Avery and how our working relationship has made me stronger in business," Grayson said.

"I swear; I didn't approve this. How did Penelope get in it?"

"I'm getting down to the bottom of this," Grayson father said, storming out of the office.

Grayson paced the floor and dialed Avery's number, but it was a waste of time. He wanted to tell her it was all a mistake, but he knew she wouldn't believe him.

The Senior Mr. Foster returned, and he wasn't happy. "Son, Penelope had changed the article before she quit. I talked to the magazine, and the change came from her, as your assistant," Mr. Foster stated. "I called her father about it, but it won't change the fact that it's out there. Avery's creditably is essentially gone

right now. I can see why she is pissed off."

"I don't want to lose her dad," Grayson said, letting more emotion into his voice than he intended.

"Son, I'd say you have the weekend to fix it all."

* * *

At five o'clock, Grayson drove up to Avery's house. *I hope Adam and Avery don't keep me waiting with Adam's hysterics and kissing Avery like he owned her.*

Avery walked out just as he was about to blow. Grayson got out of his car to help her with her bags. He opened her door and helped her in the car, then placed her luggage in the trunk.

"Miss. Dodd, thank you for being prompt. I'm glad your boyfriend allowed you to leave without the usual dramatics," Grayson continued. Avery closed her eyes and tried to hold herself together as he drove.

While he was driving, he noticed that Avery was distracted. He took a moment and glanced at her. Something was wrong. "What happened? Did someone hurt you?" he asked, a little more care in his voice than he meant to show.

Avery glared at him. Here was the man that cost had her the love of her life, and now he had taken her career. No, he didn't have the right to pry.

Avery looked at him, "Mr. Foster, my personal life is none of your concern, as you've mentioned so many times."

He could feel the emotions rolling off her in waves. He knew that somehow he was the cause of so much trouble in her life right now. Apparently, her boyfriend was upset about this business trip. Big deal, he would get over it soon enough.

If she was going to play that way, he'd go along. "Avery, we have to meet with a client in a few hours, and you look horrible. Since you don't wish to discuss what's bothering you, at least try to look presentable by the time we meet with Mr. Anderson," Grayson slipped back into his usual arrogant self.

"Of course, Mr. Foster. Whatever you want" Avery replied snidely, and then concentrated on looking out the window for the rest of the drive. They arrived at the hotel where they would be staying, and Grayson went to check in. Avery had gotten them a suite with different rooms so they could work through the night, but still have their privacy. The bellhop carried their bags to the room as they followed.

Their first meeting was at ten with an old friend of Grayson's father, so it would not last long. Avery decided to dress the way she wanted. She adorned herself with a coffee and cream double-breasted suit that screamed power. When she stepped out of her room and into the full view of her boss, Grayson was floored. He had never seen her dress this way before and was stunned with how amazing she looked. He realized that he wanted this woman.

Avery and Grayson walked into the restaurant side-by-side, and there was no doubt as to who held the power. She was pure sex. All eyes were on her, but her eyes were locked on one man, the man that cost her everything.

Mr. Anderson was tickled pink. He'd never seen Grayson looking so flustered. This girl was fascinating, and he was beginning to see why his friend had chosen her. His friend had told him about the only problem, her boyfriend, but he had also heard that she had broken up with him a month or two ago. He chuckled as the waiter approached the table and was floored by the dynamically handsome combo that waited for him there.

When the waiter came over, Grayson was being quite nice, for a change. The waiter's name tag said Max, and he began to take everyone's order, until his attention was drawn away from the list of specials that he failed to memorize and redirected to Avery. Max smiled at her, and she smiled back, caressing her hands and making him momentarily forget the waiter/customer dynamic. After dropping his pencil three times, Max managed to regain his composure and write in his own bizarre shorthand everyone's preferences for drinks, appetizers, and entrees.

Grayson was also transfixed as he stared at the young woman who was his assistant. He'd never seen her in this light.

However, she was a woman, his woman. *Whoa, my woman?*

Where did that come from? We just work together. Grayson thought as he tried to get himself together. *I'll talk to her about this later.*

They sat and chatted as they waited on their order. Max brought their order and placed it all before them. Avery made sure to thank the young man vocally, causing the young man to brighten up as he hurried away.

"Miss. Dodd, we are working here. I'd prefer if you kept your flirtation on your own time," Grayson stated, annoyed that Avery seemed interested in the guy. "Besides, I'm sure your boyfriend would not appreciate this type of behavior."

"Thanks to you and your manipulations, Mr. Foster, Adam left me two months ago. So, what I do is no longer a concern for him," Avery looked at him. "And as for our waiter, are you jealous because he seems to like me?" she asked with a smirk on her face.

"Oh dear! I am so sorry to hear that Miss. Dodd. You will meet someone else, I'm sure of it. Perhaps, you've met them already," Mr. Anderson jumped in, trying to alleviate the tensions at the table.

Grayson was mentally reeling at the news she'd just given him. She was a free woman now. Apparently, she had been for a while. Maybe he could... He looked at her face and instantly saw the hatred she felt for him.

Grayson didn't like Adam. Adam never appreciated Avery like he should have. Avery worked hard to support them, and Adam wouldn't even try to keep a job. Adam had hurt her, and Grayson would make him pay. But first, he had to get Avery to see him as a man, not just her boss. Also, she had to want him and not be turned off because he was her boss. Or because he had helped end her relationship and possibly her career. Grayson had his work cut out for him.

"Grayson, Avery, it's been a pleasure. Thank you for breakfast.

I'll relay your proposals to the rest of the team," Mr. Anderson stated as he prepared to leave.

Looking at Avery he added, "He didn't deserve you; you know. But I know you will meet someone who does."

He then smiled at Grayson,"Son, I'm going to call your father and let him know he should be proud."

Avery thanked him for his kind words before excusing herself. Fuming at Grayson again, at his audacity, Avery stood, "Excuse me, Mr. Anderson." Then she went to the ladies' room. Mr. Anderson seized the opportunity to address his Godson before she got back.

"She deserves to be treated like a queen, son. When you get her, you'd better treat her right. Do you hear me?"

Grayson faked ignorance, "Sir, I don't know what-"

Chuckling, Mr. Anderson waved off the lie, "You interfered in her relationship with that other man. You made sure she was never home. So now what do you plan to do?" Mr. Anderson asked.

Grayson stopped the professional facade, "I don't know. Man, she's hot. All I think about is her! This morning, wow! But I know she hates me. She blames me for Adam leaving, and for that stupid article. How do I..." Avery returned and Grayson stopped talking.

Returning to her seat, she bid Mr. Anderson farewell as he left.

Glaring at Grayson, Avery stood to return to their suite. Grayson followed her, determined to get a handle on the situation before it got out of control. The daggers she shot his way through breakfast told him that she wanted blood; well, he'd just remind her of who was boss.

Upon entering, Grayson decided to confront Avery about the actions that occurred this morning. "Miss. Dodd, er, Avery, I understand that you are upset about your article, but this morning was really uncalled for. You openly flaunted your sexuality by flirting with that waiter. It was unprofessional."

"Shut up!" Avery demanded. She had listened to him enough through the last two years without any arguments, but today she didn't care if he fired her. He'd listen to her today. "Excuse me? What did you just say to me, Miss. Dodd?" Grayson demanded.

"You heard me. I didn't stutter. I said *SHUT UP!* For over a year, I've worked directly for you. I ran when you called, leapt when you said jump. I gave up everything for you," Avery started pacing while she vented to him. "All I had was Adam. We had been together since college, for five years. Before you, it was only him. I told you I needed that weekend, but you didn't care. All you cared about was having me around because I work my ass off for you. Well guess what? Now he's gone. I don't have anyone anymore, I might be losing my job because of your stupid article, and it's all thanks to you. So, don't you dare try and lecture me. I'm not listening. I will do my damn job, but I want you to stay the hell away from me."

Turning to face him, Avery realized he was standing so close she could count the freckles on his nose.

Grayson grabbed her by the waist and covered her lips with his. The whole while she'd been talking, he could not help but wonder how soft her lips were. He could wait no longer and had to taste. At first, she resisted, then for a brief second, Avery responded. Her body exploded in a mass of sensations. Reacting purely on emotion, Avery's response surprised her.

"No, no, stop." Avery reacted, violently shoving him away. "How dare you? Ugh! I'll never want y..."

Grayson kissed her again, effectively ending her protest.

Despite her anger, Avery gave in to the feelings that coursed through her.

She felt his hands unbuttoning her jacket as she began to remove his. Both jackets hit the floor and his hands covered her breast, massaging them through her top.

"Wait, stop, wait," Avery protested, attempting to get a handle on her raging hormones. "This is not happening. I hate you, remember, because you caused me...Adam," she fought for a moment to clear her head. Then she pushed away from him.

"Damn it! I'm leaving."

Grayson moved to block her. "Avery, don't leave," he whispered. "Are you afraid? I won't hurt you; I promise. Stay Avery, please stay."

Grayson stood between her and the door. He wanted to explain his feelings to her. One look at her face, and he knew she would not listen to him right now, so he decided to move aside and let her leave.

Avery looked at this man standing in front of her, fuming. *Is he serious, right now? He'd be the last one I would even look at. The nerve...*

Shoving him aside, Avery walked out of the suite. She headed downstairs to the bar to get a drink. She needed something to help settle her nerves. When she arrived at the bar, she found a booth in the darkest corner of the room. For a moment, her world was peaceful. Then her quiet solitude was interrupted by her phone.

She checked her phone and saw that Adam was calling. *I don't want to talk to that ass!* Avery fumed angrily.

Grayson stood staring at the door after she'd left. *What was I thinking? That she'd fall into my arms? Pledge her undying love to me? I'm such an ass!*

Grayson walked into his room and sat on his bed. He thought about what his Godfather had said to him earlier. In his heart, Avery was his. Adam wasn't good or good enough for her and she needed to let him go.

He picked up his phone to call her and then decided to give her some space. Grayson decided to take advantage of the gym in the hotel and work out.

As he began to disrobe, he imagined Avery watching him. Slowly he removed his shirt, allowing fantasy Avery to peruse his bare chest hungrily with her gorgeous eyes. He imagined that her mouth would salivate at the sight of him.

Then he unfastened his slacks, his hard-on bursting out as if it was an animal being let free from a cage.

He let his pants drop and grasped his turgid member. He stroked himself ever so slowly, wishing it was Avery pleasuring him. As his tempo increased, so did his pleasure and with vivid images of his dream woman floating through his mind, he soon released his seed all over to the floor.

Opening his eyes and coming out of his fantasy, Grayson remembered he was alone, and she was not there. With a heavy heart, he finished undressing, cleaned up, donned his sweats, and headed to the gym. He wondered where Avery went. He hoped she was all right. She'd be back. Besides, they had another meeting at two, and if he knew her at all, Avery Dodd would be present and on time. She was truly a consummate professional.

Meanwhile, Avery was nursing a long island iced tea in the bar when the waiter from earlier walked in. He saw Avery sitting and asked to join her. "Hey, why are you sitting here all by yourself? Want to talk about it?" The waiter asked. Avery looked up and nodded at the seat across from her.

"Look, about this morning, I apologize." Avery said.

"Damn," the guy laughed, "I thought I could take you from your man!"

Avery looked at him surprised, "He's not...," she tried to explain.

"Girl, he was furious at me for taking your attention. Did you see his eyes he was so pissed off. He is cute, but my girlfriend wouldn't want me dating anyone else, so that's that. I'm Max, by the way and you are...?" he queried.

"I'm sorry, how rude of me. I'm Avery, Avery Dodd. I'm here on business with my boss, Ass-wipe, sorry Mr. Foster," Avery said angrily.

Shaking his head, Max replied, "Girl, you've got it bad for him. Make him grovel for a while and then go kiss and make up."

"Ugh! No, I don't like him like that, he ruined my relationship, he made a fool out of me at work, he has treated me like crap for years, and right now I hate him. He actually did it on purpose, hoping I would fall for him," Avery scoffed. "My boyfriend and I were together for five years, and he .... Ugh! It just makes me so angry. He left. He thinks I'm in love with *my boss*. He even had somebody else on the side," Avery stared at her tea glass.

Max smiled, "He's right. There is a thin line between love and hate. Be honest with yourself. What do you really feel for him? Until your lover accosted you, did you have a problem being with him before? I think you are protesting a little too much," Max stated as he stood up. "Hey, my break is over, and I've got to get back. It was nice talking with you Avery. Here's my number, call me if you need to vent some more," Then he went back to work.

Chapter Five

Discovery

Avery paid for her tea and walked back to their suite. Grayson wasn't there, and she briefly wondered where he was. Shrugging her shoulders, Avery decided to take a shower and rest for a while. Standing under the warm spray, her mind kept wandering to her delectable boss. She recalled how sincere he sounded when he asked her not to leave.

She'd never been with the man but found herself thinking about him. He was one fine specimen and kept his body in excellent shape. Closing her eyes, Avery imagined Grayson joining her in the shower. His strong masculine arms wrapping around her from behind as he slowly lathered her frame.

Carefully, cupping her breast, he then moves his hands lower to caress the hot area where her thighs meet.

Suddenly, Avery opened her eyes, shocked at the way she'd allowed her fantasy to go. She needed to call Adam back. What did he want? Really, he can't want anything else from me. I needed answers and maybe now I would get them.

Shutting off the shower and throwing on a robe, Avery found her phone and called her ex-boyfriend back.

The phone rang and Adam picked up on the third ring.

"Hey, Avery. I'm glad you called. I was worried about you and wanted to make sure you were alright," Adam explained.

"I'm fine, Adam. I don't understand what happened, but I'm fine," Avery answered. "I need the truth. How long have you been seeing someone else? When did it start?" she asked.

Adam took a deep breath, "Avery, you fell in love with someone."

Avery cut him off, "What in the hell are you talking about? I never cheated on you. I loved only you Adam, and you do this shit to me. Don't start with that

"You called out his name when we made love. It happened several times. At first, I ignored it, but then you started calling his name in your sleep. You started dressing up for him. You never dressed up for me. When you had trips, you couldn't wait to go. He would walk into a room, and I would see your breath catch. I'm sorry if I hurt you Avery, but we just didn't work anymore."

"Adam, how long have you been with her?" Avery asked again.

"Before you got the new job," Adam finally said.

"I paid for everything and you're an asshole," Avery hung up. *I called Grayson's name when I made love to Adam. There's no way in hell I did that, I would remember doing that. More lies, I call out his name when I'm sleeping, that I can't understand.* Avery was thinking.

* * *

It was near noon, and they had a meeting at two with the Bingham Corporation. Avery decided to select an outfit to wear to the meeting. Then she threw on some jeans and headed out to grab some lunch. As she was heading out, Grayson returned from the gym. He had showered there and all he had to do was get dressed in his suit.

"Avery wait, I want to join you for lunch," Grayson called as he saw her leaving.

Avery stopped, turned and looked at him. Thinking about what Max said earlier and what Adam told her over the phone, she secretly admitted to herself that she did find him attractive, but she wouldn't let him know that.

"I'm sorry. I really want to be alone right now, and I certainly don't want to be around you," she told him as she turned to walk out.

"Avery, please! We need to talk," Grayson called behind her.

She stopped.

"Ok, I'll wait. Hurry up," she told him, clearly agitated that he was interrupting her lunch.

They went to a small café a few buildings down from the hotel. They each ordered soup and a sandwich with tea. Grayson stared at her the entire time. He knew it was 'make it or break it' time. They talked about work until the waiter brought their lunch. Then they ate.

When they were finished, Grayson spoke first. "I'm sorry that you got hurt, but I'm not sorry he left you. I'm glad you're not with him anymore."

"Oh my God!" Avery yelled, causing some of the other patrons to look at them. "Are you serious right now?! You have some nerve."

Avery stood and marched away from the table. She threw some money on the counter and walked out. Grayson followed her, after paying for his own meal and caught up with her as she made it back into the lobby of their hotel.

They both got into the elevator and returned to their suite. It was after one and they had to prepare for their meeting with the Brigham Corporation.

Slipping back into his boss mode, Grayson informed her of what he expected, "Miss. Dodd, I understand you are dealing with personal issues right now. However, we are here on important business matters, so try and remain professional." Then he stalked off to his room, leaving Avery fuming.

Avery walked into her room and chose a different outfit for the meeting. She came out of her room wearing a loose yellow printed dress and a lacy corset. The color complemented her caramel brown complexion perfectly. Grayson came out of the bathroom with his shirt unbuttoned exposing his tight upper body to her hungry gaze.

Heart pounding and body sizzling, Avery turned away and refused to look at him knowing her desire could be seen in her eyes. How could she want him? She didn't understand, she just knew she desired this arrogant, irritating, incredibly sexy man.

Fuming at her body's betrayal, Avery snatched up her purse and started to storm out of the suite. She'd wait for him in the lobby.

Before she made it to the door, Grayson caught her by her wrist. The section of her wrist that he touched tingled. She felt sparks throughout her entire being. Her heart raced, and her breath quickened as her body hummed at his clear show of dominance.

He pulled her into a tight embrace, and she inhaled his scent. Her body quivered, as her vaginal area became aroused at the masculine fragrance he possessed. She knew she wanted him, but it was wrong. She couldn't want him, not after...

Pushing away from him, she demanded. "Let me go! What do you think you're doing?"

He allowed her to lean back, but didn't let her go completely?

"Avery, please. Can we at least talk?" Grayson asked.

"Adam..." Avery started to explain.

"Honey he's not here. I'm sorry he hurt you, but I'm glad he's gone. Please, Avery, don't deny this, don't deny us," Grayson pleaded as he pulled her close and into his embrace. Pushing down the shoulder strap of her dress, Grayson exposed her creamy skin to his view.

"Ah, damn it!" Avery gasped as Grayson kissed her exposed skin, moving up towards her neck.

Slowly he shoved her straps down her shoulders, exposing the swell of her breasts to his hungry gaze. Grayson thanked the heavens as her two bountiful mounds came into view. He slowly massaged her breast; closing her eyes, Avery loved the feel of his hands on her body.

"Avery, oh, Avery" Grayson whispered as she began to respond and rubbed her hands up and down his back.

"Look, stop," Avery said. "I'm not sure."

"Honey, please," Grayson pleaded and she found herself responding to his manipulations of her body.

Grayson moved and sat on the sofa then pulled her on top of him, "Avery, I want you so badly, but I need you to know this: I want it all- you and me together. No more women or men for either of us. Just the two of us and I promise you this, it will happen."

"Wait, I have to stop. You need to stop this, Grayson," Avery interrupted as she tried to get up.

"Finally, you called me by my name. Say it again, please," he pleaded as he nuzzled her neck.

Shocked by his outburst, Avery had no idea how to react.

Calling him Grayson just seemed natural and it felt good.

Grayson stroked her hair, "Avery, you're mine now. I watched you with him for a year. I grew to hate Adam. He didn't treat you right, and you deserve so much more."

Avery moved away from him, her body shivering with a need she didn't know she had. "Adam said you wanted me. I thought he was making stuff up," she said under her breath.

"We will talk after our meeting. But this gets settled today," Grayson declared after looking at the clock.

He moved away from her to finish dressing and they left together, heading to Brigham Corporation Headquarters.

Grayson drove in silence, but he grasped her hand and held it all the way to the meeting. At first, she tried to pull away, but he refused to let her go.

When they arrived at Brigham's, Grayson got out and helped her out of the car, taking extra care to touch her a little more than he usually would. He escorted her into the building with his hand placed securely on her waist.

Entering the building, Avery stepped away from him, severing their contact. Grayson was disappointed but understood that they had to maintain professionalism when working. The meeting with the executives at Brigham would be long and tedious. Grayson just hoped that there wasn't extra small talk or unnecessary debating. He wanted to get back to the hotel quickly, so he could have some private time with Avery.

Avery sat in her usual seat and was prepared to help him in any capacity that as needed. Grayson had a hard time concentrating, because he could not keep his eyes off his delectable coworker.

While he was giving his presentation, Avery reflected on the events that had occurred in their hotel suite. She admitted to herself that she really didn't mind his kisses and caresses.

She looked at him and for once, she didn't feel anger, just curiosity. He stood tall, powerful and virile. She wondered about his stamina and whether he'd last long and if he would be any good.

Being ever observant, Grayson noticed the faraway look in her eyes and how they had darkened into a deep green. He wondered if she was thinking about him.

At the end of his presentation, Grayson thanked everyone for listening, and took his seat. Avery sat and looked at him. He was watching her just as intensely. He had a hard time concentrating for the rest of the meeting. He was looking forward to his time with her.

The Executives and CEO shook hands with Grayson and the meeting ended an hour later. Grayson and Avery left the office after he declined the offer to join them on the greens the next morning. They headed back to the hotel to prepare for their final meeting. When they got back to the hotel, Grayson and Avery walked into their suite.

Grabbing her by the waist, Grayson pulled her into his body and covered her lips with his. He had waited long enough, and it was time to claim what was his.

Avery never knew she could feel this way. She eagerly wrapped her legs around his waist, and the dress she was wearing rode up, exposing her drenched panties to the steel hardness covered by his trousers.

"Avery, please honey. Make love to me. I promise, you will not regret it," Grayson pleaded. After a minute of no response,

he changed tactics. "I dare you. Deny you want me. Say you don't want this."

"Grayson, I-" she couldn't finish because he kissed her, clearing her mind of all her thoughts.

Grayson guided her to his bedroom and covered her body with his. He made short work of removing the rest of her clothing. Before long, she was naked before him. He stood and hastily finished undressing as well.

He kissed her lips, then proceeded to kiss every inch of her body. He nibbled on her neck, sucked her right breast as he kneaded the left. He then moved his attention to her left breast.

Avery was a washed with feelings. When he reached the apex of her thighs, Avery froze. Only one person other than herself had touched her there, Adam.

Grayson kissed her legs, thighs, and pressed his face into her pubes and inhaled.

"Open your legs for me honey. Let me taste you," he commanded gently.

Avery parted her thighs and he saw how wet she was for him. The darks hairs covering her sex were drenched as her scent perfumed the room. Spurned by desire, Grayson had to taste, so he licked her slowly.

"Ohhhhh myyyyyy Gooooood!" Avery screamed as Grayson pleasured her in ways her former lover never even thought about.

Grayson licked her slit, slowly inserting his tongue as he tasted her sweetness. Finding her nub, he sucked it into his mouth as a thirsty man drinking water. Avery loved it as she eagerly humped his face.

Before she knew it, she felt a familiar burning in her lower stomach and knew she was cumming. "Oh shit!" she exclaimed as her orgasm rocketed though her body.

Grayson continued to drink her nectar as it flowed freely from her body into his mouth. Crawling back up, he held her as her tremors subsided.

"Grayson, I've never...," Avery was speechless and breathing deeply. "Wow!" she then leaned over to kiss him, tasting her essence on his lips. Slowly she massaged his chest and stomach as her hand continued to drift downward. Finally, her hand felt his cock.

"Oh!" Avery gasped. It was huge. "Grayson, it feels so big," she told him with an awed voice. Slipping her hand into the waistband of his boxers, she gripped his member and pumped her hand ever so slowly.

"Ahhhhhh!" Grayson groaned as her tiny hand circled his throbbing member.

Avery rose above him, "Wait, I want to see it." She moved closer to his member to get a better look.

"Wow, it looks bigger than...," Avery gasped.

"Don't! Don't say his name. Don't mention that bastard,"

Grayson growled. "I promise; you will forget him tonight." "Sorry," she whispered. "Can I taste you? I've never..." "Please, honey. You never have to ask," he answered excitedly.

"I don't want to hurt you, tell me what to do," Avery whispered.

"You won't hurt me. Just do what comes to you naturally," he whispered.

She stroked him and saw a glob of pre-cum ooze from the tip of his erection. Avery was curious and slowly licked the tip of his cock. Grayson hissed.

She started to pull back, when she saw his face and that was all the encouragement that she needed. She took his head in her mouth and began to suck him in earnest. Her mouth felt amazing to him, and he was so close.

Then she stopped. Looking up at him she asked, "Can you tell me how to make this good for you?"

The sight of this beautiful woman kneeling before him almost made him climax.

"Listen, open your mouth and let me put it in just a little," he instructed. Slowly he pumped in and out of her mouth as she used her lips and tongue to bring him pleasure.

Before long, his balls clenched, "Oh god Avery, I'm close." He pulled out of her mouth just as Avery grasped his pulsing rock. She began to stroke him up and down, faster and faster, waiting to see what she had never seen before. She wanted to watch him climax. Grayson's moans grew louder more intense, which only made Avery pump him with wild abandon. She couldn't believe how turned on she was knowing what she was about to make him do, what was coming. Cum he did, more than he ever had before. It was on her up her arm and even a little on her face.

Holding each other in a glow of lust, Grayson smiled knowing that he finally was with the person he always wanted. "Avery, you're mine. You are my woman now. I never want to let you go," he whispered and felt her stiffen.

Avery froze, thinking she was supposed to hate him. Avery moved to get out of the bed. He stopped her. "Wait, you're not leaving. Avery, honey, wait. What happened? Please, don't leave. Talk to me."

"Grayson, I'm sorry. This shouldn't have happened. I'll have my resignation on your desk Monday morning. I'm so sorry," Avery said as she grabbed her clothes.

Grayson was stunned. She was perfect for him, and he could not let her go. Especially not now that he'd tasted her.

Grayson got off the bed and grabbed her arms to stop her. "Honey, stop. Listen to me. I know you're scared. I never thought I'd get to be with you, please don't leave."

Avery closed her eyes, but stopped trying to leave, "Grayson, I don't know. I dated one guy in high school and… I met Adam in college. He's the only person I've been with. I don't know how to please a man. Adam didn't like foreplay and he would never let me touch him like you let me touch you. He wouldn't let me see him come and you're bigger than him a lot bigger… I'm not sure."

Trying to hide his laughter, Grayson quickly embraced her, happy to learn he would be the man she would learn from.

"Avery, honey, look at me. Don't run from me. Let me love you, Avery. Please, give me a chance."

She wanted him. She recalled what Adam has said and realized that he had to have known all along that she had feelings for this man.

Adam knew that she'd end up being with him, even told her she would this weekend.

"Don't think about him," Grayson pleaded. "He has nothing to do with us."

"He told me I'd be with you this weekend. He knew," Avery shook her head in wonder. "How did he know?"

Grayson sat on the edge of the bed and pulled her into his lap. She sat facing him, placing her legs on each side of his thighs. She kissed him. Grayson needed no prodding as he actively participated in the kiss.

He reached behind her and grasped her ample bottom. Slowly he slid his hands between her thighs and began to stroke her.

She slipped her hand to his member and grasped his cock.

Then he removed his hand and she removed hers. He pulled her close and pressed his hard cock against her pussy. Avery slid against his cock, reveling in the feel of it against her burning flesh.

Avery suddenly needed to be filled. Raising up, she placed his cock at her opening.

Slowly, she pressed down as he entered her. She'd never had a man this size inside her before and was overwhelmed by the feel of him.

"Damn, girl! You are so tight," Grayson sighed.

"Ahhhh! You're so big. I feel so full," Avery gasped.

Slowly they both began to move. Grayson was determined to make this good for her. He took his time, pumping slowly, in, out, in, out, in, out.

Avery felt a pressure deep inside. She knew only Grayson could relieve the pressure, "Grayson, I need! I need!"

He quickly reversed their position with him ending up on top. Lifting her legs and placing them over his shoulders, Grayson pounded her burning pussy.

Avery never came so hard in her life, and Grayson soon followed. No one ever made her feel the way Grayson did.

She never wanted to give him up.

Grayson held her after they made love. He knew that he'd never let her go, but he didn't want to rush her.

Realizing the time, Avery started to get out of the bed.

Grayson wrapped his arms around her to stop her.

"Honey, where do you think you are going?" he asked nuzzling her neck.

"Grayson, you have a meeting with the Blanc Corp. President at six. It's four o'clock now. We're here to work, remember?" Avery reminded him.

"Damn, alright. Will you wear that suit you had on this morning? I loved you in that suit, damn!" Grayson whispered feeling his cock grow hard again.

Avery noticed, "No, no Grayson. We have to get out of bed."

"What about later, honey?" he asked, pouting a little for effect. "Can I taste you later? I want to lick your slit, suck on your clit, and drink the juices out of your pussy, please," he asked as his hand rubbed between her thighs.

Avery spread her thighs a little to give him better access. "Yes, later, I promise," she sighed. Grayson smiled as he fingered her into a quick and short climax. At 5:30, Avery was dressed in her coffee and cream suit accompanied by Grayson who was dressed just as professionally.

After a short wait, the hotel valet drove up. Grayson held her door open as she got into the car. He held her hand as he drove to the Blanc Corp. headquarters. "For good luck." he said as he kissed her knuckles, before they got out of the car.

Chapter Six

Returning Home

The meeting with Blanco was short and precise. Within two hours, Avery and Grayson were headed back to their hotel.

"Hey, are you hungry?" Grayson asked. "We can stop and grab dinner."

"Yes, please, nothing fancy though. Let's go to a local diner," Avery suggested.

So, Grayson drove to a local eatery. Entering, the couple selected a seat, and a waitress came and took their order.

While waiting for their food, there was no talking. They simply enjoyed the show a local band was putting on.

Grayson needed to touch her, so he reached across the table and grasped her hand. Avery gripped his hand back and they sat there holding hands, just enjoyed being with each other.

Smiling, Grayson stared at her as he held her hand.

Avery looked at her boss, her lover, and she blushed. She could not believe what had transpired today.

"Grayson, what does this mean? I mean, does this extend beyond Texas, or not?" Avery asked. She valued her privacy and wanted to know if he was serious about her, or if this was just a quest for him.

Placing his finger over her lips, he whispered, "If you think I'm letting another person, man or woman, near you, think again." Then leaning in close he, whispered, "I see I need to brand that pussy again, so you'll know it's mine."

"Grayson!" Avery squeaked as the waitress came to set down their drinks.

From the smile on the girl's face as she walked away, she had heard him. "Grayson, she heard you. Oh my God," Avery declared embarrassed.

Laughing, Grayson moved closer to her ear. He loved making her blush. "Sorry, I'll behave. Why don't I let you punish me later?" he suggested quietly.

His deep voice conjured up some fantasies that Avery had about him but dismissed as foolishness. He watched her and saw her eyes go dark and smoky. His semi-erect cock came to full attention.

What is she thinking? It had better be about me and not anyone else. Grayson thought clearing his throat to draw her attention back to him. "Oh, sorry. Zoned out for a moment. Excuse me," Avery said blushing again.

"Um, honey," Grayson whispered, "Whatever it was, promise not to hurt me too much."

Avery smiled sweetly, "Who says I was thinking about you?"

"Honey, you can think about anyone you want, as long as you understand that only I can touch you," he replied proudly.

Avery crossed her arms ready to argue, but he stopped her with three sentences.

"Avery, it goes both ways. You are the only woman that will touch me in any way. I'm yours," he whispered.

"Fuck, where is that damn waitress with our order? We need to hurry," Avery whispered hoarsely under her breath.

She then rubbed her neck, drawing Grayson eyes to its length and beauty. She didn't have a single mark on her beautiful skin. Tonight, he'd fix that; she was his and he'd make sure everyone knew she was taken.

Avery squirmed in her seat, as her body yearned for the man sitting in front of her. This man had her center flowing with juices.

Avery closed her eyes and took a couple of deep breaths. Grayson knew she needed him. He needed her too. His cock was rock hard, and he was sure it had turned purple at this point.

Avery opened her eyes and looked at him. She saw the same level of intense arousal in his eyes as she felt. He was breathing hard.

"Grayson!" she whispered.

"Let's eat and then I promise, you won't feel your legs in the morning," he kissed her hand.

The waitress returned with a bag in hand and a grin on her face. "Can we get those to go?" they both asked together.

"Already have the to-go boxes right here," the waitress said as she placed the bag on the table. "Have fun." She left with a wink and a very big tip.

As soon as they made it to Grayson's car, Grayson lifted Avery and she wrapped her legs around his waist as he sat her on the top of the hood.

The feel of him pressed against her opened a firestorm inside Avery and she needed him right then. Grayson pulled back.

"Honey, we've got to stop. We'll be at the hotel soon." But she was grinding her pussy into him and then she jerked.

Grayson held her close as the power of her climax rocketed through her body. Soon she calmed down and they drove back to their hotel.

Grayson kept his hand on her waist and guided her back to their suite.

As soon as they entered, Avery undressed. Grayson loved her body—he was mesmerized by her beauty.

"Fuck Grayson, get naked now. I need you," Avery demanded.

Like a good boy, he did what he was told. As soon as he removed his boxers, Avery knocked him on the bed and straddled him. She rode his member hard, causing Grayson to scream out.

"Oh God! Girl, where did you learn that? Good God! Damn! " Grayson lost all coherent thought.

Avery yelled out in kind. "Grayson, you feel so good. Oh God, you're so big." Moaning, she rolled her hips on him, grinding herself into his thick bush at his crotch. The hairs of his crotch teased her, causing her to quiver.

Avery screamed "Grayson, oh God Grayson!" As she came hard and fast, she engulfed every inch of his rock-hard member.

The clenching of her center on his cock pushed Grayson over the edge. His hips surged upward on her downward stroke driving him inside her even deeper.

They came together and it was bliss. Grayson held her tightly and then realized his chest was wet. Avery was crying.

"Honey, what's wrong? Did I hurt you? Oh God honey, I didn't mean to hurt you," Grayson tried to move away from her so he could see her face better.

"Honey, I'm alright. It was just so intense," She took a deep breath. "I've never experienced something like this with anyone else," Avery admitted. Grayson relaxed as he realized he hadn't caused her any pain.

Grayson stroked her hair. She always kept it up, and he didn't realize how soft it was. "It's alright Avery. It's supposed to be like this. I've dreamt of this for months, and I never thought I'd have a chance with you."

"How long... how long have you felt this way?" she asked.

"Since the moment I laid eyes on you three years ago. I came to your floor to see your supervisor. You were at your desk typing. You wore your hair longer then. When I saw you, my heart stopped," Grayson stared off lost in a memory.

Grayson decided to confess. He wanted her and he didn't want the past or his actions to interfere with their future. So, he continued. "That day when you were leaving work, I got in the elevator with you. I didn't speak because I couldn't think of anything to say. When you got off the elevator, you met Adam and embraced him. I hated Adam in that moment because I wanted you to be mine," he inhaled. Avery pulled away slightly; she braced herself for what he was about to say.

"I tried to forget you, but I kept making people miserable. All I could think about was you, your smile, your skin, your hair. Honey, you're perfect."

He gently ran his fingers across her brow and down her cheek. The confession continued. "My assistants kept quitting because I was in a state of perpetual horniness and only you could temper the blaze. The last assistant that quit was an older woman that was near retirement. She told me I was an insufferable, conceited, hardheaded, know-it-all who had no compassion or remorse for those who were forced to work with or for me. Then she spoke to my dad and told him the same thing, which made him even more upset. The sad thing is that she was right. Dad decided to find someone for me and told me I'd better not run that person off. Why he picked you, I don't know, but I was glad he did."

Grayson stopped for a moment and looked at her, "When you walked into my office, I smiled inside. But I had to keep my tough façade. You were working with me. One day, I asked you to stay late, and you called him. The two of you exchanged words and he made you cry." Avery gasped. She had no idea that he was aware of the disagreements she'd had with her ex-boyfriend.

"I wanted to be with you all of the time. So, I started making up stuff. My desire for you permeated my brain. You were all I could think about," he confessed. "Adam said I wanted you, and he was right. I've always wanted you."

"Grayson...," Avery whispered, but he silenced her with a kiss and continued.

Avery walked to his bedroom door, then turned and looked at him, "Just give me some time," she walked to her bedroom.

Grayson, the meanest, toughest, orneriest, most difficult man was shaken to the core as he watched her walk out.

Avery got in the shower, tears streaming down her face, as she washed her body. She wanted to believe him, but what if this was just another conquest for him? She also owed Adam a true apology because he had told her the truth. He knew what her choice would be, even before she knew she had a choice. Avery got out of the shower and dressed. Then started to think better of it. Adam had cheated on her first. She didn't owe him anything.

The next morning, it was time for them to check out, so Avery gathered the rest of her things and finished packing. She knew Grayson was packing as well. They would talk on the flight home. Grayson Foster was hers and she knew she couldn't be without him.

Grayson was terrified. He didn't know what to expect. She had to care about him. She wouldn't have responded like she did if she didn't. The bellhop came and carried their bags and placed them in the car. She and Grayson walked to the front desk to check out. Neither spoke. The flight home was tense, and quiet. Grayson was afraid that she would say they were done. Avery was thinking that Grayson had changed his mind about them.

At three in the morning, Grayson pulled into his driveway. Avery woke up and recognized that they were at his house, not hers.

"Grayson, I need to go home," she whispered.

"Honey, you are home. I bought this house for us," Grayson exhaled. "I wanted to give you things he didn't and ..."

"Oh, Grayson. How could you buy a house for us? I don't understand," Avery stated perplexed.

"I don't see why you're confused, you decorated it," Grayson answered seriously. "Come in and let's go to bed."

"What do you mean I decorated it?" Avery demanded. Then she recalled him having her hire an interior designer and selecting the furniture for the house and everything in this house. Grayson had paid all her student loans for the work she done on this house.

"You may be my boss, but you can't order me to go to bed," Avery said, hands on her hips.

Grayson loved her fire. She had taken his shit before, and he could see she wasn't about to let it start again.

"Damn, honey. I love it when you argue," he answered pulling her close. He kissed her, effectively ending her protest. "Now, let's go to bed."

He led Avery to his bedroom and carried her to his bed. He laid her down gently and kissed her. Slowly he undressed her and kissed every inch of her delicious body.

Soon she fell asleep. Grayson chuckled. His woman fell asleep while he was pleasuring her. That could mean one of two things. He was either that damn good, or that damn bad.

He quickly disrobed and joined Avery in bed. The bed he never planned to sleep in alone again. The next morning, Avery was up before Grayson and in the kitchen talking with Mrs. Lopez when he found her. Grayson walked in and kissed her soundly. Mrs. Lopez cleared her throat and smiled. He was happier than she'd ever seen him.

Eventually he did drive her back to her house so she could dress for work.

He walked her to the door and waited in her front room. While standing there, he realized he had never seen the inside of her house. Curious, he walked down the hall to her bedroom.

He knew this was the bed she shared with Adam, and an overwhelming need to burn it engulfed him.

"Hey, what's your problem? I can call a cab if you're in such a hurry. You insisted I go home with you last night," Avery joked. "Yes, I finally get you in our bed, and you fall asleep on me," Grayson teased her right back.

"That's because you're that damn good," she smiled. "You loved me so well I couldn't help but sleep."

"Oh, really?" he pulled her to him, kissing her slowly.

"Grayson, we have work. We have to go to work," Avery reminded him as she struggled to pull away while she could still form coherent sentences.

"Let's call in sick today," he whispered nuzzling her neck as he led her toward the bed. Soon, she was in her bed with him on top of her. He kissed her and slowly opened her blouse exposing her bountiful lace-clad breasts to his hungry eyes.

"You're not sleepy now, right?" he queried. Avery's body was on fire, and she was no longer thinking, only indulging in the feel of his hands on her body. Before she could answer, he stroked her breast and pinched her nipple.

"Oh God," Avery moaned.

"Oh honey, I'm not done. Do we get to skip today?" he asked chuckling.

"Fuck, we've got to be quick. You have a meeting at nine. Undress, now," Avery demanded.

Grayson laughed, "You're so demanding. You want me naked, undress me."

Avery stopped. Then, looking in his dark eyes she saw a challenge. He brought her to the edge so easily. It was time to return the favor.

"Um, Mr. Foster, I really don't need you naked. Besides, we don't have time for all of that," she whispered. Slowly she unbuckled his belt and opened his slacks.

Her hands slithered inside and brushed his rigid cock. It was Grayson's turn to become eager and overheated.

"Fuck Avery! Don't tease me girl," Grayson hissed.

"Up," she ordered. He raised up and she pulled his trousers and boxers down.

Avery was kneeling at his feet, when she looked up straight at his thick pole. The sight of her kneeling beside his cock, made Grayson leak pre-cum from his hard member.

Avery leaned down and licked his pre-cum off his cock. "Oh God, Avery!" Grayson groaned.

Avery stood and removed her pants. Climbing on top of him wearing only her shirt, she straddled him and slid down his stiff pole inch by agonizing inch.

"Oooooooooooh," Grayson groaned as he felt her heat surround him. Then she moved. She rode him softly until he begged for more. When he tried to move and pick up speed, she stopped. "Fuck, Avery. Don't stop," Grayson ordered.

"Mr. Foster, I'm in charge right now. So, stop ordering me around," Avery whispered as she had his entire cock buried up in her.

"Avery, please. Honey, please. I need it. I need you," she raised up and down, still pumping him slowly, teasingly.

"Fuck," Grayson yelled as he quickly reversed their positions needing with him on top between her creamy brown thighs.

Grayson started pumping into her furiously. He could only grunt and move. The feel of her hot sheath had him teetering on edge.

Soon his balls clenched as Avery yelled his name. Her pussy clamped his cock in a rapturous vice, and they came together, each fighting to catch their next breath.

Grayson collapsed on her but eventually moved to her side, "Avery, I have one more order for you. Clear our calendar after the meeting this morning. We have another trip."

"Wait, no. You don't have any other trips scheduled until the thirteenth," Avery stated. Since she scheduled all of his appointments, she knew when he had to travel.

"Listen to me, I'm going to talk to Dad after the meeting, then after that we're flying to Vegas. This time tomorrow you will be Mrs. Grayson Foster. Don't even think about refusing me. I'm not going to live without you, Avery."

"You can't order me to marry you. Grayson, everything cannot always go your-" she tried to explain.

He kissed her, "Avery, it's bad enough we have to explain to my dad why I need a new assistant."

"Wait, what does my job have to do with anything?" Avery asked, confused.

"We won't get any work done. And public nudity is illegal. I'd have you on my desk naked every day," Grayson explained. "Besides I want Grayson Jr. to have my name before he arrives in nine months.

"I'm keeping my job," Avery stated. "If you want me to marry you then I get to keep my job."

"Fine have it your way," Grayson said. "Then we are putting in a daycare center in the building."

"Works for me."

Chapter Seven

Nine Months Later

"Grayson Foster, hurry the hell up. I want drugs, lots of them! You're never touching me again. Owwww! This hurts," Avery complained as her frazzled husband Grayson drove her to the hospital in an entirely reckless manner.

Grayson had already called his dad and he was meeting them there. They arrived at the hospital and Avery was taken straight to her room. The doctor examined her and told the nurse to prep for delivery.

Eight hours later, Avery was holding her son, Grayson Owen Foster, Jr. in her arms and he was perfect. Owen came in and met his new grandson. The old man was overwhelmed. The baby was clearly strong, and he knew with his son's genes, he'd be tough little kid.

Soon, the nurse came in and suggested everyone leave and let the new 'Momma and baby' rest for a while. Grayson put Grayson Jr. in his crib and escorted his dad and their friends out to the lobby.

When he made it back to the room, his family was fast asleep. He kissed his son, and then walked over and kissed his wife. He sat in the oversized chair by her bed, grasped her hand, and then he too fell asleep.

Welcome to The Jade's Inn Family Excerpt

Second book in Jade's Inn Series

"NEED YOUR HELP!" Julian's panic-stricken scream echoed through the halls of Jade's Inn. You expect to hear shouting in a place like this, even though sound-proof walls, when inhibitors are left at home. But you don't expect to hear a scream from a man like Julian, a scream laced with the unmistakable sound of fear.

I wasn't back from training vampires in Texas for an hour when Julian's plea for help brought Sam and I to our feet. "It's Johansen, he is attacking the family," Julian cried breathlessly.

Before I came back to Jade's Inn, I saw this, all this in a dream. I had hoped that's all it was, a dream, a nightmare brought on by two-day old pizza and a zombie movie marathon.

I already knew the answer to the next question, but I asked anyway, "Where is this happening?"

"Half a block around the corner," Julian said.

We built Jade's Inn together. Julian and I, friends that rats and cockroaches would be embarrassed to be seen with. Now it's a beautiful hotel, and I feel like I'm risking my life to defend it.

There was a soft rain greeting us, like a mist coloring the world gray. By the time we turned the corner into a darkened alley the rain began to pour. Out of these sheets of rain we could see Johansen and his followers... and there were a lot of them.

I did not recognize all of them, but some I did. I just wish I didn't. They were the outcasts, the banished, and the ones who had broken one of our more solemn laws by drinking the blood of humans. It changes them. Once they taste human blood, they're hooked, addicted, and willing to do anything to get more.

There were too many to count, I was sure that there were far more than we could see. I was also sure all of them could see us. We kept our backs to each other, watching as another set of shadows stepped out of the rain.

There was a collective sigh of relief once we realized they were not the enemy, they were family, ready to fight by our side.

There was a moment of silence but for the sound of rain falling on a city that had no idea what was about to happen.

The silence ended.

The war began.

They were the first to move, and they moved quickly, but not quick enough. On a normal day, and this was anything but normal, Sam is one of the kindest people you could meet. This gentle giant had two of these invading vamps by the throat. Their lifeless bodies hit the rain-soaked ground; their throats still remained in Sam's clenched fists.

Julian was faster than all of them, having been blessed with strength. It was as if he moved between the raindrops, lashing out against his foes, bringing them down before they even have a chance to be afraid. The younger members of our family held their own. Christopher, a young man who, days earlier, called everyone he knew to brag about leveling up on some war game, held his enemy to allow Michael to drive a stake so far into his chest that it came out the back. John, Julian's older and much larger brother, was blessed with strength, which he was putting to effective use by cleaving off the heads of those stupid enough to attack him.

"It's good to have you back, Aramis," John said. He and his sword were covered in blood, just as I was. There was so much blood that it impossible to tell how muchours was and how much was theirs. I remember years ago when John taught me that if a vampire attacks you, break his neck. He'll still live, so you can interrogate him. If you want them dead, however, remove their head, or the heart. Today we weren't going to be asking them questions.

I had to admit it was hard to witness all this violence, even harder to be a part of it. Then I heard a scream. It was distant, but I would recognize it anywhere- my brother, Charlie. There were two figures caught in a fierce, brutal battle, and while it was difficult to see them through the sheets of rain, I knew one was my brother.

I struggled to make my way towards him, but before I could get there, one of the combatants fell lifeless to the ground. The victor stood above the fallen, and continued to strike without mercy, without humanity.

"Charlie!" I screamed. He was still at a distance, but I could see him when he turned around, wiping the blood out of his eyes.

"What's wrong with Charlie?" I asked John.

"It's been hard since Elizabeth came into her gift," he answered coldly. Elizabeth is Charlie's daughter and long story short Elizabeth superpowers have given her father a run for his money.

The family fought well, they were trained well, I should know...I trained them. But the blood of the enemy was on my hands to. I didn't keep the numbers in my head of my own victories, my own collection of hearts and heads. However, as the unofficial, official head of security for the family I would need a body count before the day was done.

I have taught many in the family that if the fight cannot be avoided, at least he aware of your surroundings. Don't just look but listen. It's helpful when your opponent tries to attack from behind...just like the one that was coming up from behind me now. Whoever he was, he clearly had never taken my classes. If he had, he would have avoided the puddles of water. I ducked about half a second before he lashed out. His blade missed, mine didn't.

Another heart to count among the dead. The sounds of battle died down. The driving rain was no longer driving. Through the clearing air I could see Dominic, the undisputed leader of the families until upstarts like Johansen try to undermine everything he built. He was caring for two of the young members of our band of vampire soldiers, Josh and Jaren. He was tending to their injuries, wounds that appeared very serious. Josh had the worst injuries; he was lying unconscious on the ground while Jaren struggled to remain on his feet, guarding over his twin brother.

Jaren's hand was pressed tightly to his side like a broken dam, trying to hold back the blood. I began to move to him, to help him to find a quiet place to heal, but when I saw an enemy vampire, one we thought was dead, race towards Jaren, I began to run. Before I could get close enough to help, Jaren found his strength. He bolted forward, and with one swift move, seized a bloodied blade from the cold grasp of a dead vampire and imbedded it deep into the skull of his assailant. As nature would have it, the rain was only taking a breather, and it returned with a vengeance. At first, I thought it would keep the innocent onlookers indoors, but I found I no longer cared who saw us. I just wanted this ended, and it could only end with Johansen's death.

His name is Chris, he's one of the younger vampires of our clan, and one of the most impulsive. He has talent and potential, but he was no match for Johansen, as the excessive amount of blood indicated. He was still alive, but if he was going to stay that way, I needed to move fast.

I moved fast. Dominic moved faster.

"This family will be mine," Johansen shrieked, warning the world. Famous last words, at least in the vampire community. Dominic entered the stand-off with his rival carrying two swords, he used the first to pierce the heart of this enemy, the second to send his head across the darkness alley and into a puddle of mud. It was a fitting end.

You always hope that with the fall of the leader his followers will...follow. Their mission had failed. Their goal could no longer be achieved. But did they lay down their weapons and raise their hands?

Of course not.

The rain poured from the heavens, and the thunder began to rage, as if God was sending a message, I hoped they all would stop and listen.

They didn't.

Fueled by what I would guess was a misguided sense of revenge, they fought on, dying for a dead cause. The battle raged on, otherwise gentle people reverting to savagery. The brutality was becoming unbearable...Until...

"STOP!"

The deafening sounds of fighting and dying were gone, and now the air was thick with an eerie silence that you could feel deep down into the marrow of your bones. The only thing worse than the unsettled silence was the overwhelming stench of death that made this unimaginable war all too real.

It had stopped—all of it just stopped. The nameless, faceless horde of bloodthirsty vampires lie dead, strewn throughout this remote back alley. I could see the faces of my family, my friends, and even strangers who fought at our side. We were all looking at each other, looking for answers, as we stood battered, bruised, and bleeding, hoping the rain would go away like the reality of what just occurred.

Some of us began to tend to the wounded, while others undertook the morbid task of collecting the bodies, and the body parts of the fallen. The question of why this happened was not the mystery that plagued our thoughts, there was only one question.

"Was that...did you hear Elizabeth in your head?" I asked John.

He was holding someone's leg at the time. He paused before answering, "Yes."

"Put the remains in that bar over there," Julian said. "I'll be right back," It did not take him long to return. He had a grimace on his face and the ankle of a body he was dragging behind him. It was easy finding our way into the vacant, run-down bar. Julian stepped inside, still pulling his lifeless victim behind him. With an effortless flick of the wrist, he sent the body flying to the middle of the floor. "He managed to get into the Inn unnoticed and tried to kill Caprice." "How did he die?" I asked.

"Fell off the roof of the Inn," Julian said. I didn't ask anything else, and he didn't tell me anything else, but I really wanted to meet the girl that Julian had found for his soul mate. We moved all the bodies into a bar so that it would look like the bar had caught fire and burned down, instead of a vampire burning.

The pile grew until the last body was laid on top. It was then doused with a special accordant before some of the family gathered together, encircling the grotesque heap of death. In unison they lit their matches, and when Charlie's match highlighted his face in the darkened room, I saw an expression of a killer in his eyes that I had never seen before and hoped would never see again. Others in the family lit matches, and they all dropped them ceremoniously on the pile. Within a matter of seconds, the pile was engulfed in flames. Dominic would have called the fire department by now. The rain, while helping to keep the smoke down, could not put out the raging inferno of the bar. I could feel the heat on my face.

The smoke billowed out of the bar, followed by the weary soldiers that I guess could be called the victors. Most of the family members had rushed our wounded to our own little emergency room. The rest of us took our time, feeling the heat of the flames on our backs as we made our way through the ever-growing crowd of curious onlookers. We were all thinking the same thing once we heard the sirens in the distance. The remains of our enemies would burn down to nothing, including their bones. The police and fire department would assume students from the university broke in on a dare, or part of some offbeat hazing ritual, and couldn't hold their liquor glasses.

The fire burned quickly, very quickly. In a matter of moments, the bar was coming down on the pile and the fire department was there. We all left to help the others. I still didn't understand what had happened with Elizabeth and her telling everyone to stop, and why it worked. What was going to happen?

The house that Charles's lives in was as busy as any hospital emergency room, but with drastically different patients. The basement of his home has served as a make shift hospital for many years, treating the kind of wounds that would be difficult to explain to ordinary doctors and nurses. The blood and pain distracted everybody from the thought that was plaguing the back of their mind.

What had happened?

Was that Elizabeth that we all heard?

We were all curious. We all wanted to know. Well, I'm sure there were some who didn't want to know, didn't want to face that reality. Then there are some who would insist. They're called the Presidium. They are the law and security within our ranks. I had no idea why they weren't deployed to the battle, but the man who would know was Brian Quinn, and he was standing about ten feet in front of me.

"Quinn, why weren't you there?" I asked in a loud whisper.

"I was told to remain behind by two of the elders," Quinn explained. There was frustration in his voice, it was subtle, but it was clear that he didn't like explaining himself.

"Well, I can keep things under control here, so you can go home," I offered.

"If I recall, Aramis, you are not officially back until tomorrow,"

Quinn pointed out. "Besides, I have one more thing to do before I leave."

"Why didn't the Presidium show up?" I asked knowing they were called.

"What's going on?" Julian asked.

Quinn has always taken a great deal of pleasure and pride in knowing things that others do not. It's the source of the smugness he wears like a badge of honor. I really hated that guy. He wants only power and would sell his birthright to get it.

"...and the Presidium?" I asked again.

"The Presidium was...otherwise occupied. I had orders, like you."

"Those orders may be moot when Charlie finds out," I said still keeping my voice low but stern. "Your position may change."

The grin on his face was confident if not sinister. He walked away and I followed at a discreet distance.

Elizabeth was standing in the driveway, watching the taillights of a car disappear in the night. I kept a close eye on her, but I wasn't alone. Jaren, one of the twins, I could always tell them apart by the way they stand and move. I was keeping an even closer eye on Elizabeth. The first to step out of the shadows was Quinn.

"Is there something you want Mr. Quinn?" Elizabeth asked.

"Good evening, Miss Elizabeth," Quinn replied. His greeting was hollow. He had never spoken to Elizabeth directly before, and I have to say, when he did, he made it sound chilling. "I wonder if you would mind accompanying me?"

"What? Where?" she was confused and scared, but who could blame her?

Quinn didn't respond.

Jaren did.

Within a blink of an eye, Jaren was standing between Elizabeth, the girl he loves, and Quinn.

Jaren's eyes locked on Quinn, while Quinn glanced up, looking past the young man to the SUVs pulling up the long driveway. When the occupants of the ominous black SUVs stepped out, it was like they stepped out of a bad Hollywood remake movie with black pants and a black, tight skinned shirt that showed all their muscles. This was not the normal uniform. The Presidium showed up hours after we fought for our lives; if I didn't know better, I would think they were on government time.

The pistol I carry with me is pretty much useless against a vampire, since you have to put enough rounds into the heart to obliterate it.

Also, I didn't have any rounds. But Quinn didn't know that when I pulled it out and put it at the back of his head.

"You touch her Quinn, and I'll kill you."

Quinn turned to face me; my pistol was now pointing right between his eyes. "You heard her." His voice was stern, as usual, but with a hint of something new...fear. "Do you understand what she did?"

"I just spent the better part of the day putting vampires out of my misery," I said with absolute resolution. "I've developed a knack for it. One step toward her, and I'll kill you and anyone else who gets in my face." Maybe it was the look in my eyes or the blood on my clothes that kept the others at bay. "Now, let's talk."

Quinn's expression did not change. It never does. "I'm listening," he said.

"Who called for this...for her?"

"The Elders."

"Why? What Elders?"

He hesitated, as if he was considering taking a bullet rather than divulge any information. "Carter... and Johansen," he conceded. "They want her locked up until we fully understand what she's capable of."

"Two elders," I said. "And one of them just had his head severed from his neck. Who else? That's only two; I want to know the other four. Now."

Jaren was able to keep his composure, swallowing his quiet anger. Then it came back up. When he spoke, his voice was calm, in a very grownup way. "My grandmother would never have approved of this," he said in a way that made it sound like if we gave him five minutes alone with Quinn, he would take this Quinn's head off. This was his job. I had the random thought that Jaren was going to make a great enforcer when he gets older, before I focused back on the gun pointed at Quinn's forehead.

"Show me the order," came the thunderous voice of Dominic. Charlie, Julian, and others who fought with us from the Presidium stepped out of the house. As Dominic walked up to Quinn, I lowered my gun and stepped aside, letting him through.

"There was no written order, Dominic," Quinn said. "There wasn't time. I was told to pick her up."

"You're trying to take her without any written authorization?" Dominic asked. "It doesn't work like that." By this time, he and Quinn were standing toe to toe, each waiting for the slightest twitch, a mere flinch that may be regarded as a sign of weakness.

"Is there going to be a fight over this?"

"No more fighting! Please!" Elizabeth cried as in yelling at everyone. You could see Elizabeth tears fall as she just wanted everyone to just stop. Her plea was followed by a stressful silence that was finally broken by the sound of a cell phone.

"Dominic, my grandmother wants to talk to you," Jaren said handing him a cellphone.

Dominic expression looked confident; Quinn's suddenly did not. "Yes," Dominic said. "Yes, I see. Thank you," he returned Jaren's phone without taking his eyes off Quinn.

"It would appear that she did not contact you," Dominic told Quinn. "She authorized nothing. We know Johansen didn't call you, because he's dead. So, this is what's going to happen, tomorrow we are going to have a meeting about this and about Elizabeth, but you will not be taking her with you. The Elders are aware of what's going on. Mikayla Campbell is coming down to do some work for them; she has a list of people to see and you're at the top of its Quinn. Tomorrow at ten. Elizabeth, you'll be there too."

That familiar, uncomfortable silence returned, but this time it was shattered by an unfamiliar voice. "She killed my father!" I did not recognize the voice or the young man who stepped out of the SUV.

"Then I assume your father took part in the fight we just had," Dominic said. "A fight that you missed. Your father chose to follow Johansen, a mistake that he paid for."

The young man did not move, did not speak. His eyes conveyed anger, but it was his trebling lips that indicated he was truly freighted, too scared to raise his voice and object. Charlie did not take his eyes off the young man as he reached into his pocket and withdrew a cell phone. He didn't dial a number, just hit one button.

Quinn's eyes grew narrow with suspicion. He slowly took out his own cell, but try as he might he could not get it to turn on. "I'm locked out!"

"You all are," Charlie said. Despite his statement, they all tried their phones, tried and failed. "You are all locked out of the Presidium too. Do not attempt to leave, your key codes will no longer work on these vehicles." Charlie then raised his hand. It was an unusual gesture that made everyone, even Quinn, back up a step. We all turned to hear the sounds of more vehicles approaching. More SUV's, carrying more Presidium. Everyone turned back to Charlie as he continued talking, "You have violated our laws, defied orders, and you attempted to apprehend my daughter. You will stand before a tribunal tomorrow to answer for these crimes."

More soldiers of the Presidium exited their vehicles and stood by waiting. "Take these men back to the Presidium and hold them for the night," Charlie ordered. These new prisoners began to follow the soldiers; however, it immediately became obvious that Quinn wasn't going to go so easily.

The move was slight, nearly imperceptible, but Quinn did move, as if to reach for a hidden weapon behind his back. Julian, however, did notice, and had Quinn's hands cuffed before he could take a second breath. This brief disturbance gave one of Quinn's men the chance to draw his own hidden weapon, point it at Elizabeth, and fire.

This time it was Jaren who moved with unimaginable speed, putting himself front of my niece. He had to love her to step in front of a bullet. He was prepared to take the bullet. The bullet stopped one inch from his forehead.

We all watched in disbelief as the bullet slowly turned around and then quickly embed itself in the left eye socket of the man who fired it. If I had not seen that for myself, I would never have believed she did it.

"Jaren, get Elizabeth inside, now," Dominic ordered. "Do not let her out of your sight and do not let her outside."

"She dangerous," Quinn insisted. "She needs to be eliminated." With his hands cuffed behind him, Quinn was not able to defend himself when Jaren's fist landed squarely on his chin, sending Quinn to the hard, rocky driveway. With fists still clenched, Jaren took Elizabeth inside.

Charlie made no attempt to help Quinn to his feet, but instead crouched down to look Quinn in the eye. "If you can justify killing someone because you believe they are dangerous, perhaps we should consider just how dangerous you are to this family. Even your own mother was dangerous. You are aware, as we all are, that Elizabeth is mentioned in her grandmother's journal as one day leading this family. It's not hard to see the motive behind anyone who would wish her dead."

Quinn said nothing as he managed to stagger to his feet. He didn't have to say anything, we all knew what was on his mind, what was always on his mind. He wanted to lead the Presidium. I wouldn't be surprised if Johansen had put him up to this. I'm gone for two measly months, and when I return, part of the Presidium is trying to take down the Main Family. What the Hell! "Someone needs to tell me what's going on," I insisted.

"Not here," Dominic said. "Let's move inside to the dining room table." Before entering the room, we could already hear Elizabeth as she cried. "What's the matter?"

"Syd...Sydney is in trouble," Elizabeth sobbed. "Her dad...he's hitting her."

"How do you know Elizabeth?" I asked. "I mean; you've been though an awful lot today. Maybe you just need to..."

without warning, she grasped my hand and held it tightly. At that moment I saw it all, slaps with open hand and savage strikes with a closed fist. With each blow, Elizabeth gripped my hand harder, as if she was feeling it to.

With such brutality, I couldn't help but think of my sister, an enforcer like me, or...she was. She died at the hands of one of our own. It was senseless and brutal, and I should have been there. I wasn't and now her husband is trying to raise their little girl all by himself in California. Now I see my brother-in-law beating her own daughter, but he wasn't just beating her, he was killing her.

"We need to get some there, now" I said.

"We will," Dominic said. "What she saw may not have happened yet, in fact I know it hasn't. Elizabeth, sweetie, why don't you go get some Tomato juice." We call blood 'tomato juice' because it's easier to hide it among people not our kind. "Okay Grandfather," she said and went to the kitchen.

"Right now, we need to talk about the Presidium," Dominic continued. "There were members of the Presidium that turned against us. How far does it go?"

"Here you go Grandfather," Elizabeth interrupted quietly as she placed a large pitcher of blood and a stack of plastic cups on the table. "Tomato juice anyone?"

"You go ahead, sweetie, drink as much as you need," Dominic told her. "Then I'm going to need your help."

"My help? For what?"

"I need you to take us to the Presidium," Dominic stated like it was this easy thing to do.

"I've never been there," Elizabeth said. "Dad always said no to it."

"I know," Dominic reassured her. "You won't have to leave this table."

Elizabeth looked nervous, even frightened. She reached for Jaren, who took her hand and sat beside her. She began to relax. Clearly, Jaren had a calming effect on her. I was very impressed with Jaren, the way he handled himself today. He is clearly more mature than his nineteen years. I'm not sure where his twin brother Josh is.

Josh, Jaren and Elizabeth- their story had become wellknown in certain vampire circles. Our people choose their soul mates at a very young age. Elizabeth found Josh and Jaren, she chose them, and they chose her, but she's only supposed to choose one. For now, she's choosing to down another glass of A positive.

"Now Elizabeth, I want you to think of the Presidium, concentrate on them," Dominic said in a quiet, soothing tone when she had set her cup down.

"But Grandfather..."

"You can do this," he encouraged. "Don't think of them the way you saw them today. Think of them just two short days back, see them in your mind. Now everybody, hold hands." We joined hands...and nothing happened.

"Try again Elizabeth," Dominic said. "Think of Alorah's father and Mr. Quinn, two days ago."

I could feel Elizabeth tense up at the mention of the name Quinn, but it seemed to work. The room grew dark, and when we could see again, it wasn't the dining room. It was a council room. We were in the Presidium.

We could hear the muffled voices of ten people sitting around a conference table. The highest ranking one was Quinn, and he seemed to be doing most of the talking. I recognized a few others, people who shouldn't even have access to that room. The indiscernible chatter continued until the meeting was called to order. Even without the chatter, we were seeing and hearing everything as if through a fog.

"Mr. Quinn, you may receive a phone call in a couple of days, a call to action. When that call comes, you must ignore it. Once Dominic has been eliminated, I will take over leadership of the families and you will become head of the Presidium." It was the unmistakable voice of Johansen.

"If you lose?" Quinn asked.

"In that unlikely event, you must get a hold of Elizabeth. Take her away. Lock her up. If she taps into the power, I believe she has, we will lose, and lose big." Johansen rose to his feet and began to circle the table "By the time the rest of the Presidium discovers what's going on, we can kill the other elders and control everything."

The fog lifted, leaving all of us at the dining room table, staring at each other in astonishment.

Julian was the first one to speak, "What happened?"

"I'm...I'm sorry, Grandfather, I can't keep it open," Jaren quickly poured her another glass of tomato juice.

"Relax, sweetie, you did great," Dominic told her. "Why don't you go up to bed. Jaren, help her up the stairs and then come straight back down so Charlie doesn't have to go up and get you."

Elizabeth clung to Jaren like a life preserver as they made their way upstairs.

"You need to get to Sydney's home," Dominic said to me.

"Before it's too late."

"I'll leave tonight," I said. So much for sleeping in my own bed.

"Aramis, I need you back in a month or two," Dominic said. "I miss having you around."

Chapter One

Two Months Later

Never again! That's what I have promised myself. Never again would I allow myself to fall in love. It had been an easy promised to make. The pain of Sean leaving me was indescribable. I thought he loved me. No words could do it justice, but in my most cold and detached moments, I admitted to myself that under different circumstances, I could have moved on. I feel like I've been turned into something ugly, something broken, and something not entirely me anymore. If I didn't have bossy friends watching over my every move,

I would move out of this area and start over, but I still have Caprice and Geri. I wouldn't want to leave them, they're like my sisters. They're the only people who have stuck by me through everything.

Of course, I had been a fool to believe someone like me could be loved, that I could have an emotionally healthy relationship which lasted more than the length of a contract. I might as well be living in the third circle of hell, thank you Dante. Besides, he had only liked me because he hadn't really known me. If he had ever seen me, the real Dawn, he still wouldn't be around. He

would have run from me as if I were Satan carrying a pitchfork, down with in a pit with you! I would have let him go like I should have done when I had the chance.

So, never again. That's what I had promised myself. Promised myself over and over again. Pushed even the hint of love away at every turn. But no matter how hard I pushed, it found me once again.

This moment found me in the doctor's office, one of the happy steps on the way to a contract. Contracts aren't a traditional form of dating, but it has worked well for my best friend Caprice and her hot, handsome beau Julian. I have to admit; I have been reaping the benefits of being best friends with the girl who has been hooking up with one of the owners of Jade's Inn on a nightly basis.

Poking and prodding while playing doctor is a lot more fun than the real thing, especially the prodding. So many memories, so many positions...

The benefit here is that I am being poked and prodded by Caprice's doctor. He's the best. He definitely knows his way around the female body, and when he touches you, you almost feel like he can do more than just examine you, it is like he can see into your soul.

After peeing in a cup with numbers on it, while being watched by an ever-vigilante nurse with squeaky shoes and an adorable overbite, we were off to x-rays. This was a first for me, having my body lit up by radiation. If the EKG is any real indication, my heart is beating the way it's supposed to, but those electrodes can be put in some real personal places. I'll have to keep those in mind next time I do the "naughty nurse" routine.

After all that it was quiet time. That's the time when they drop you off in the exam room, and tell you the doctor will be right in. I didn't count the minutes as much as I did the cautionary posters of sexually transmitted diseases, followed by the number of birth control pills in my purse, which, by the way, wasn't nearly enough. My count was interrupted by a knock.

"Hello, I'm Dr. Benjamin A. Jensen," came the voice from the opening door. "I have been informed that you work at Jade's Inn. Is this correct?"

"Yes, for the last eight months," I replied as I watched him stroll into the room without looking up from his clipboard. He was an odd sort of a man who looked like this science guy I saw in a movie once, with long gray hair that was tied back. I couldn't help but like the guy, I mean, he's as old as some of my professors, but none of them look this good. If I was married to this guy, we would be playing doctor every night. I know when most girls think of older men, they're like "Eww." But for me...wow. An older Cary Grant and an aged Sean Connery, now that's a threesome I can get into.

"So, tell me miss..." he began.

"Just call me Dawn," I replied, so glad that he couldn't hear my wicked thoughts.

Even though he kept his eyes glued to the clipboard, I could see just a hint of a grin. "It says here, Dawn, that you didn't know your parents," the doctor said.

"I have no idea who my dad is," I admitted. "My mom died while I was in foster care."

"Is this your mother's full name?" the doctor asked, holding the clipboard so I could read it.

"Yes," I said, glancing at the clipboard. "I think she died from drinking too much." There was no emotion in my voice, like a casual conversation about last night's thunderstorm. But then I thought about it. "No one at the Inn will know I was in the foster care system, right?"

"I wouldn't be concerned, only the owners read the files," he reassured me. "So why isn't your last name Campbell?"

"After my mom died, my foster parents adopted me," I said. "Nice of them, until they divorced two months later and sent me back into the system. I mean, who does that? You send back a bad Philly steak and Swiss, or a tacky t-shirt with reindeer on it, not a kid."

"Sorry sweetie, I don't know the answer to that," Dr. Jensen said with genuine sympathy.

"I know who does it...people who don't give a shit in the first place. People who just want the extra cash and then fight about what to spend it on." Another knock on the door ended my tirade before I got too carried away. An attractive young nurse, whose hair was somewhere between red and blond, came in and handed some kind of paperwork to the doctor. My first thought was 'Wow, I have that outfit at home,' I have this bad habit of saying what I think. I just hope they didn't hear me.

The nurse, whose name tag said 'Talia' walked over to me and first gave me a hug and then her card. "Call me if you need anything," she said. I'd been hit on by women before, but Talia didn't have that I'm-up-for-it-if-you-are tone in her voice.

"There are two things we need to discuss," Dr. Jensen said as he sat down. "First you have a vitamin and mineral deficiency. There is a mineral shake that I want you to try. We have what you need here, and I want you to make one every morning and drink it all."

"Why is this happening?" I asked.

"Basically, you're over doing it," he said bluntly. "You're taking a full load at school and working at the Inn. I've been told by Sam that you do more than just...entertain, you also help out by painting the rooms. That's a lot of activity. It takes a lot out of you."

"Are the shakes chocolate?" I questioned.

"Yes, some are," he responded.

"Okay, Doc, you talked me into it," I said, sighing sarcastically.

"What's the other thing you wanted to talk to me about?" "Well, this is just an offer," the doctor said.

Oh no, where's he going with this? I thought.

"I would like you to do a DNA test," he said.

Okay, not what I thought.

"There are several Campbell families in this area," he continued. "It might be possible to determine if you are related to any of them, even distantly. If you are, I can learn more about your medical history."

"When I was in foster care, I was told there were no other family members around here, but if you want to try Doc, go ahead," I said, sure he would not find any family members, and I wasn't really sure I wanted him to.

* * *

I doubled over as Frank delivered a crushing blow to my abdomen. My throat ejected blood. I spat it out bitterly.

"Stay down!" Frank growled.

"Fuck you!" I grunted. I was hurt, exhausted, beaten. But I looked up at him with loathing as I forced my wobbly legs to lift me up to my feet. I felt my head spin, but I would not give up, not for my niece, never.

Frank kicked my legs out from under me just as I got to my feet.

I dropped face first to the ground. I hadn't expected to be tripped, and my face hit the ground hard. I bit my tongue when my jaw hit the floor. I looked at his feet.

Frank kicked me in the ribs. "Beg me to stop, Aramis," Frank roared. He kicked me again. "All you have to do is beg."

Something happened then that I couldn't explain. There I was, bleeding from the mouth, one eye nearly swollen shut, nose bleeding. One of my ribs was broken and sticking out of my chest. I could barely stand on my own. And I started to laugh.

It started out as a chuckle, but to Frank's fury, I began to howl with powerful fits of laughter. Frank kicked me again and again and again, somehow making me laugh harder and harder with each kick.

I felt Frank lift me by the scruff of the neck, setting me up for a kick in the head.

I looked up at Frank. Even as I was roaring with laughter, my hatred showed in every line of my face. To my surprise, Frank let go.

"Psycho..." Frank muttered, shaking his head as he closed the front door behind him, taking off in his car.

My laughter slowly died down to chuckles. I had won.

I had told Sydney to hide in her closet. I could hear her crying through most of it. She's sixteen and Frank had caught her kissing a boy on the back porch and had a fit. Well, she almost kissed him. The poor guy barely made it out of the house alive. I showed up in time to keep Frank from killing the both of them.

She cautiously peeked around the corner and saw me lying there on the floor.

I was truly a sight to behold. I was strong, very strong, but Frank was stronger. As soon as I found out why I was so weak, I would be going after Frank and taking Sydney with me.

Sydney knelt down next to me.

"Sydney," I groaned.

"Hey Uncle, " she said, smiling down at me sweetly.

"Check it out! I showed him who boss!" I cackled.

Sydney wasn't amused. You could see it in her eyes. "Want me to get you something?" she asked quietly. She hadn't realized it, but she'd been holding my hand... which suddenly started to sweat. I always get really hot when I heal. "No, give me twenty minutes. I will be healed."

"I hate this," she said.

Frank had only ever hit her once, since I had been there. She yelled at Frank about his temper, and he hit her, hard. The incident landed her in the hospital.

A month ago, I made sure that Frank never laid a finger on Sydney again. Frank hated me, so it wasn't that hard. I was ordered to come and live with him until the human blood was out of my system. I know Dominic sent me here to protect Sydney and to stop me from wanting to kill Brian because I really wanted too! So far, it was working.

"Uncle?" Sydney came back with an armful of everything, a pillow, water, a bowl for spitting blood into. She put a pillow under my head and started running her fingers through my hair. "Aramis, are you okay?" No response. "Uncle Aramis,"

Sydney said. "Oh my god! Aramis! Aramis!"

"I'm fine, just give me a minute," I told her.

Then I heard my Sydney's voice again, "Uncle? Are you awake?"

I wanted to respond, but it seemed so far away, almost as if I'd just thought the words, or remembered them.

"Uncle?" Sydney was here. "Uncle I need you to wake up okay?"

I opened my eyes.

Sydney was sitting by my side, crying into her hands. She still didn't understand what we were, but she would someday.

"Chin up sweetie. What's got you so blue?" I asked.

"Uncle, OMG!"

She hugged me painfully and told me she loved me.

"Where's your dad?" I asked.

"Not sure," she said.

"You need to go to Mikayla's house and tell her dad what happen, go now and stay there."

"I can't leave you here by yourself," her voice shook. I lifted my still functional arm and took her hand in mine, rubbing it gently with my thumb.

"Go now," I said. Sydney got up and left.

Before long, I closed my eyes and allowed myself to rest. I was hurt worse than I thought. After a while, I don't know how long, Jeff was there, handing me some blood.

"Is Sydney safe?" I asked.

"Yes, she's with Mikayla and Tina," Jeff said. "Sleep. I ordered different blood for you." Once again, I closed my eyes, and despite the pain, I slept.

* * *

Dear Diary...is that what I call you. Maybe I should call you my "Dream Lover" because what I'm dreaming about is you. That's why I'm going to start writing this, to get my head around the fact that this is only a dream and I need to stop daydreaming of a dream guy that is only, well...a dream.

Kurt left when the contract was done a month ago and Sean signed up for another six months. I was pretty happy, but a week into the new contract I was told by Sam that Sean got a job out of state and had to move. He paid up for the six months and I'm getting a weekly paycheck for doing nothing. I work at

Jade's Inn. It's a brothel, but not a normal brothel. We have contracts and there are the one-nighters too. I haven't done that yet. My friend Caprice and I are known as Courtesans at the Inn, which sounds classier than some other names.

The money is really good and sleeping with the same guy for six months is like being in a real relationship with them. The job gave me more time to study for school. I want to be a teacher one day, and trying to handle four jobs last year almost killed me. The only problem is you can't date outside of Jade's Inn and right now I'm not sure what to do. See, Sam told me I could be put back on the web to find someone new, but I will lose the money I'm getting from Sean. So, the only way I can keep getting the money is to do one-niters, which isn't always as much fun as it sounds.

I also paint murals on the wall of some of the themed rooms. The money there is good too, but I have to pay for school, fees, books, rent, and food. I just don't have the money after getting a new used car.

Okay, enough self-pity, back to the dreams. It's not like it was a flavor of the month off of a firemen calendar. I've been dreaming of the same guy for three months that I have never seen in real life, only in my dreams. The sex is beyond amazing. We are always having sex, but sometimes I wonder if I'm in his dreams, instead of him being in mine. I dream of doing things I've never done in my life, and I dream of love that is so great I didn't know it could be real.

The first dream was like an introduction.

We were sitting at a table. I have no idea where it was, and I guess it doesn't matter. I think it must have been some kind of sidewalk cafe. The table was very small, really just large enough to hold two cups of coffee. We were sitting across from each other. My dream guy was wearing a black polo shirt. When I see him in my mind, he's wearing that shirt. In some of my dreams, he's naked, because one of us has taken that top off.

As you can imagine, I like those dreams. I like to think of him, naked in my arms, our passion building as we make love. I like to think of him, naked beside me, as we recover from the exertion of our sex. I like to think of him, nude, holding me as we share a tender kiss. I like to think of him, naked, quiet, a faint smile on his lips, cuddling me as he sleeps.

We were sitting at that little cafe table, talking. For some reason, we had agreed when we planned this meeting that we would not touch each other, even to shake hands, until we had finished our first cup of coffee together.

At our table, we talked, we laughed, we swapped stories and opinions, It isn't long before we know that we were meant to be. It has only been a short time, you know, and yet it seems like we've loved each other all our lives. We kept drinking our coffee. We were all alone, together, and every second was better than the one before. We could see each other. We could say anything we wanted to, and no one could hear us. No one interrupted us. No waitress came by to refill our cups, but they never got empty. After a while, we talked about that, wondering how that could be. We couldn't touch each other until we had finished our coffee — that had been the plan. We had made an agreement, a promise to each other, so we couldn't touch. We've promised to always keep our promises, so all we could do was talk. See what I mean, I think of him as a real man not a dream.

It was a beautiful time. We talked for hours, and I loved him for every word he said, but I was getting impatient for his touch. Frankly, I was getting sick of coffee, and he seemed to be, too. Regardless of how much we drank, we couldn't empty our cups. Have you ever had a more frustrating dream? One in which you couldn't do something important, no matter how hard you tried? That's what I felt. I was so frustrated by the situation, and there didn't seem to be anything I could do.

In my dream, I told him I needed to be held, and he said he wanted to do that, but that we couldn't do it until the coffee was gone. I started to cry, and I was desperate. My Dream Guy had to do something. He had to fix it. So, he did the only thing he could think of to do, he grabbed both our cups and dumped them on the ground.

We looked at each other, and my tears had stopped. In fact, it looked like I had never been crying at all. My Dream Guy was smiling at me just as broadly as he had been before I started to cry. He asked me if we could be together now, and I said we should try. Then, at the same time, in the slow motion we sometimes have in dreams, we reached out our hands toward each other. For an instant, the tips of our fingers touched... That's when I woke up.

I don't usually remember my dreams in such detail, but this one was more vivid than any I've ever had. I've never tried to write down my memory of a dream, but I had to write about this one because this was only the beginning. I never wondered before about the origin or meaning of my dreams, even though I know that some people put a lot of effort into explaining dreams and finding their message. This dream was different. I had to give it some serious thought. I didn't mind. In fact, I loved doing it, because it was a dream about my Dream Guy.

Some of the symbolism in this dream is obvious. I think Sigmund Freud would have a field day with these dreams and would probably say I just need to get laid.

One of my early fantasies involved meeting in the coffee shop of a motel somewhere and deciding whether we would get one room or two. I think that waiting to finish our coffee could symbolize me waiting for the "right man" to meet. The fact that we couldn't finish our coffee, no matter how hard we tried, was a symbol for the longing and the fact that we still haven't made the move to find the one. If you can't tell, I'm taking a psychology class this semester.

I've decided that the fact that I woke up when we first touched is also symbolic, in a good way. I think our first touch will be so exciting, so thrilling, that it will jolt me awake from the blue funk I've been in for quite a while. That started the next dream and the next. My dreams get more and more erotic as I dream them, and now I'm having daydreams of my guy.

I'm tired of waiting for Mr. Right. I know I can be strong enough now to work around the obstacles of not having a guy in my life. Now, I have to go back to bed. I had to write this down, because I didn't want to forget a single detail. I had to share it with you, and now I have.

Chapter Two

EVERY TIME I FALL asleep, I dream of Dawn, the girl of my dreams.

Sadly, I don't think she is real.

Dawn lowered a hand to my cheek, and started absentmindedly running her fingers through my hair.

She leaned forward until our faces were inches apart. She stopped for a moment, just to look at me so close for the first time. She lowered her lips to mine. She stopped and looked down at my beaten face; I was in a bed and Dawn was taking care of me. She pulled herself onto my bed and shared a pillow with me.

"Aramis?" Dawn asked.

"Mmmmmmmm?" I moaned to acknowledge her.

"Could you hold me?"

Dawn opened my arms, and she lay her head against my chest. Fortunately, all of my broken ribs were on the other side of my body, or she would certainly have woken me up in agony.

"Aramis?" Dawn whispered.

"Mmmmm?" I moaned again.

"I love you," Dawn said.

I opened my eyes to make eye contact with her. "I love you too gorgeous." I kissed her on the forehead and closed my eyes again.

Something's wrong! Dawn thought. *I'm not supposed to feel like this!*

Dawn couldn't stop the feeling. She felt a wave of love and lust rush through her. Just sitting there, letting me hold her like this was, well, perfect. I never wanted it to stop. Her heart

was pounding like hooves on a racetrack.

I give up! Dawn thought. *I can't fight this anymore. I need you!*

I wanted the dream to be sweeter and changed it to Dawn standing on the front porch of my house in Lava Hot Springs, watching the sunrise. I wanted to turn away, but I just couldn't take my eyes off her.

I just stood there, watching her gorgeous light brown hair blow back in a morning breeze. Her eyes were closed, and she spread her arms to catch the cool wind. She was smiling. A storm was coming, and I knew how much she loved the rain.

She was beautiful. I'd known this in the back of my mind for as long as I could remember. Her eyes were a stunning bright blue. Her skin, soft and slightly pale. Her warm smile could stop a man's heart. She was tall with curves that made her look like a model. She had that perfect hour-glass figure, that I would swear measures thirty-six, twenty-eight, thirty-six. She had a certain elegance and beauty about her that I couldn't stop thinking about, no matter how hard I tried.

A man could easily fall in love with her, I thought, trying badly to look away, still hiding my face in the shadows.

Dawn looked back into the house. When she saw me watching her, she smiled adoringly back at me. She didn't know I was there at first, she just felt me watching her.

"Come on out here Aramis! It's goanna rain!" she yelled; voice filled with excitement not natural for so early in the morning.

I stumbled out of the house, hating the butterflies in my stomach.

We just relaxed for a while, letting the wind rush across our faces, feeling the rain drizzle down on them.

"I forgot how much of a morning person you are," I said.

"I forgot how much of an owl you are!" she said, observing the shadows under my eyes.

I laughed. I had always was a bit of a nighthawk. We started talking about movies and music. I always loved classic rock, grunge, and metal. Dawn was more into modern hip-hop, and even (to my dismay) 80's music.

Then the conversation moved on to girls.

"Are you and Stacy still having sex?" Dawn scowled. I shook my head in exhaustion "What's wrong with Stacy?" "I just think you could do better," Dawn said.

"You always think I could do better. Who do you think I should be with?" I asked.

"I don't know, someone more like...," Dawn trailed off.

"Like what?" I said.

"Like me," she said with the cutest smile in the world.

I smiled back, "Dawn, if I met someone like you, we wouldn't be having this conversation."

The sky turned dim. Clouds blocked all but a few rays of sunlight, and the rain started to pick up. Dawn paused.

She grabbed my arm and rested her head to my chest. I felt my heart start to pound. "Why didn't you tell me you felt that way?" she asked me.

"Felt what way...," I started before she cut me off with a kiss.

Her lips were smooth as silk. Her kiss sucked all the oxygen out of my lungs. I froze, but quickly gave in as I lost control of my senses.

I felt light-headed when she slowly slid her tongue into my warm mouth. I instinctively massaged her tongue with my own. She began to moan into my mouth. She gently pulled her body closer to me, grinding her crotch against my leg. She ran her hands under my shirt. She opened her mouth to gasp for air, never taking her lips off mine.

I broke the kiss, and quickly shifted away from her. 'You're not real, only a dream,' I thought.

She smiled again and gave me a quick peck on the lips. I didn't move. Our eyes met and I knew what she wanted. She wanted me so badly; she'd do anything for me.

"Dawn..." I breathed.

Boom! Thunder shook the house and the rain picked up even more. This was going to be a serious storm. "Aramis come find me," Dawn said, "I'm real." "Where are you?" I asked.

"Home...your home," Dawn said. "Come home."

"Home," I mumbled as my eyes opened. I was no longer looking into the eyes of Dawn. I was looking at a pillow. I recognized it. It was mine; I could tell because I keep telling myself I need to wash it, but I always forget. I painfully turned my head, looking up at a light that was a little more blinding than I remember.

"I need to go," I grunted as I sat up. "I'm taking Sydney to my brother's, or I guess she can come stay with me."

"Wait, you need to know this," Jeff said in an ominous tone that was meant to keep me seated with all my groggy attention on him. "I tested the blood that Frank has been giving you.

There's human blood in it. From what I can tell, he drained the blood from the body after it was dead." At this point, Jeff began to pace the floor. "I don't get it. Why would he do that?"

"Because he knows me," I said. "He's been hitting Sydney, a lot. He knows I will kill him as soon as I get my power back."

"You stay here," Jeff said. "I'll go talk to Sydney. If what you say is true, you can take her with you." With that he turned and left, and I just fell back on the bed. I could feel every bruise, every wound.

It was going to take me longer than I thought to heal. I closed my eyes. I wasn't dreaming. I wasn't even asleep, but I was in the mind of someone else.

* * *

"Fuck you too! Asshole!" I yelled at some faceless driver cutting me off and then flipped him the bird for good measure.

I managed to arrive at Jade's Inn without taking a life and was greeted by Sam, but without his usual smile. "You don't have to do this," he said. I couldn't decide who he sounded more like, my father or my psych professor.

"C'mon Sam," I pleaded. "I haven't worked since Sean left. I thought I had enough money to get me though summer semester before I had to do this type of work again, but with having to buy a new used car, I just don't have the money for books."

"Why don't you wait until we put you back online," Sam suggested. "You don't need this one-night stand. This isn't really your style."

"Thank you, Sam, you're sweet, but this one-night stand will get me the money I need. After this you can put me back online."

"I understand the money is good," he continued. "I just feel that this is the wrong way to go about it." His look was stern, but I shrugged, and Sam sighed. "Okay, this man will not talk.

He takes what he wants and leaves. That's it."

"Good to know," I said. "Do I need to dress in anything special?"

"No, what you're wearing is fine. You'll be paid well to let him...do as he pleases. Are you sure you're up to this?"

"Sam, I'll be fine," With a sigh and a great deal of reluctance, Sam walked me to the door of the room where my mystery date awaited.

"I've seen girls leave in the middle of this just because of his unique taste," Sam warned.

"I can do this," I reassured him. I opened the door and closed it behind me, leaning up against it. I was feeling more nervous than usual after Sam's warning. I just have to turn off my feeling until after this. I haven't had a one-night stand since I was a freshman. I looked up and saw him. He was huge.

By huge, I mean he's 6'2" and well-muscled, but he was also vaguely familiar. He was even more familiar once he was standing right in front of me. He reached out, gently running his fingers up my sides as he slowly lifted my shirt up my stomach, over my breasts and finally over my head. It flew across the room, followed by my bra after he unhooked it with one hand.

His hands were warm when he cupped my breasts, "Don't be afraid, I won't hurt you," he said but I felt chills when he lightly teased my nipples. I began to squirm under his touch before his lips met mine. It was a gentle kiss, soft at first. It came intense. He tore his lips from mine, moving swiftly to my breast, licking, sucking, even biting gently. He quickly moved to its twin, giving it equal time.

This familiar stranger did not lack for passion; I'll give him that.

He was bald, and not just a little. A first for me. I felt tiny compared to him, he had to stoop pretty far to reach the breasts that he seemed to enjoy so much. As much as I loved the attention, I took the opportunity to remove this man's shirt while he was so conveniently bent down. Of course, his muscular definition was more pronounced. This guy looks like he could bench press 300 pounds easy. That's it! I finally recognized him. He's a bouncer at the Bloody Rose. I've seen this guy carry a redneck under each arm like they were made of empty beer cans.

I loved the skin-to-skin contact when he lifted me in his arms. He held me for a moment, looking into my eyes, without saying a word, before moving me to the bed. He brushed my lips with his fingers before kissing me again. This bouncer really knows how to kiss. I wonder if he learned that here.

While this man would be considered an Adonis by any woman with a pulse, I just kept picturing Aramis, my dream guy. I imagined it was his chest that I was touching. My hands circled and squeezed his nipples before traveling up to his massive shoulders, down his arms, finally coming to rest on his waist. The top half was bare; it was time to work on the bottom half.

First was the belt buckle, followed by the button of his jeans, they were easy and quick. The zipper, I took my time slowly lowering it, then pulling his pants open just enough to move my hand inside to stroke the very heart of him. I took my hand away only for a moment, but it was long enough to bring a sigh of frustration. My fingers reached around to take a firm grasp of his firm ass. The cheeks felt soft, supple, yet strong enough to crush coal into diamonds.

I pulled his pants to the floor and froze. He was big, and this time I was not talking about his height. Now I know why the girls left. He was scary big. Then he put his hand under my chin and lifted my head up to him. "If you can't handle it, I understand."

I took my clothes off very slowly and very seductively. So, there we were nude, marveling at each other's...nudity. God he was gorgeous, and so proportional.

My eyes were mapping and memorizing every square inch of him, and there were so much to look at. His eyes were doing the same to me, until he glanced across the room at a bottle of wine sitting patiently on a table, already open.

I admitted that I was still thinking of my dream guy as I walked to the table was more of a sexy saunter meant to keep his attention on my body. I poured the wine into two tall glasses. With another sexy walk to keep his attention on me, I made my way to the bed and handed him one glass. He took the glass, I sipped from my glass, and he did the same. I turned around and downed the rest of the glass of wine licking my lips after. I reached up and kissed him and I could still taste the wine.

One of the perfect moments for me is to have my lips locked with a gorgeous man and feel his gasp when I reach down and grab his cock for the first time. The good ones never pull their lips away.

I slide my fingers down to the base, and back up again. I began to stroke harder, faster, hoping he might say something in the heat of passion, even a plea to his favorite deity, but he didn't utter a word.

He did seem amiable. He let me do whatever I wanted. Once our lips parted, I put my mouth on his chin. I began to nibble and lick along his jaw, down his neck, his chest, and his welldefined abs. I was on my knees once I felt the tickle of his groomed hair. I now had a close-up view of the largest penis I have ever seen outside a John Holmes who in the porn movies and who has the biggest penis. The first time I saw a John Holmes movie was at a friend's house. I never knew a man could be that big and the guy in my dream was really scary big. In a dream he didn't scare me as much but in real life that's another story.

There was a look in his eyes, an anxious look, waiting for what I was going to do. With a firm grasp of the base of his long shaft, I kissed the tip before running my tongue underneath to his balls. My tongue ran back up the entire length before circling the head over and over. Then, with some effort, I took him into my mouth. I have to admit, I love giving guy's head, and I've gotten really good at it, but there was no way I was going to take all of him down my throat.

My pace quickened, my grip tightened, and he began to squirm just a little. When I gently cupped his balls and began to tickle, he squirmed. I pressed my thumb to the sensitive spot underneath his balls and began to caress, sending him over the top. As my head bobbed up and down, I stroked this spot in time with my movements until he couldn't take anymore and pulled away.

He pulled me to my feet. He pushed me up against the wall, bent down and took one nipple in his mouth, sucking strongly, while his other hand was pinching my other nipple. Then he switched his attention. Suddenly he dropped to his knees, pulled my legs apart, shoved one leg over his shoulder, and kissed my center, followed by his tongue that seemed to have a mind and a mission of its own. I thought my legs were going to give out on me. He grabbed me by the ass to hold me still and buried his face deep in my center. He licked, he bit, and he sucked. Lord, he couldn't seem get enough of the way I tasted. Finally, he shoved two fingers into my pussy, clamped his lips around my clit, and sucked for all it was worth. My climax was instant. I came, and came, and came. I had never experienced anything like it before. I slid down the wall to the floor. My legs just couldn't hold me anymore.

He lifted me up, carrying me like I weighed nothing, and gently put me on the bed. He came over to me and kissed me. He reached over on the bed stand, grabbed a packet and opened it up. Jade's Inn has always provided a wide variety of condoms, in different colors and textures. I love it when the guy chooses the one, I like. "Allow me" I took it from him and put it on him, which made him smile. It was the first sign that he was enjoying himself. He hovered over me, lifted my hips, and then slowly pushed forward, an inch and stopped, allowing me to get used to his size. If he went in fast, I would have had to leave because he would have hurt me. He knew he had to take it slow so my body could handle his. I could tell by the look on his face that he was concerned. "Keep going, just be slow so I can handle all of you," I said.

I wrapped my arms around his back and held on. He started slowly, pulling all the way out, then all the way in. Lord, he was a tight fit, and it took a while before my body relaxed from how big he was. He was slow at first, giving me time to get over the size of him. After a few minutes he increased his speed. My hands stroked up and down his back. I just held on for the ride. Then without even a step, he rolled over into his back with me still inside him. I found myself on top. I sat there for a second, savoring the feel of the new position, and how deep he was, then I started to move, a little at a time. I leaned toward him almost touching his chest with mine to catch my breath not all the way down on him, which sent him even deeper into me. He didn't move, letting me have control of what I could handle. I reached down and rubbed my clit, riding him as fast as my body would let me as my climax approached. I exploded. I couldn't keep my pace anymore.

He lifted me off of him, then rolled me onto my stomach, lifted my hips into the air, and entered me from behind. I gasped; I didn't think I could take too much more of this. The feel of my climax finally sent him over the edge. He shoved into me, grunting with his release. Finally, sated, he pulled out of me. He collapsed with exhaustion.

"I want you again," he said. I didn't even have the strength to answer him. He laid down next to me, pulled me into his arms kissed me. Without another word, he rolled off the bed and got dressed. A tear came down my cheek with the voice in my head came to me, reminding me of Kurt and Sean, the ass who told me he cared for me and then left me. There's just one thing about one-night stands-they're only about the sex, and I had needed that, but after came the pain of what you just did. I haven't felt this bad since I was a freshman and I thought we were going to be together, but after the sex he left too. I laid there wondering why I couldn't find a guy who wants me like the guy in my dreams. I know why, because guys like that are one in a million and Caprice, my best friend, had already grabbed him.

* * *

"That son-of-a-bitch is sleeping with my girl!" I yelled. I was livid once I realized I was back in my own head after seeing my dream girl working on her back at my themed hotel. She was with another man while questioning if I was real, and I was torn. I wanted to find her, but I needed to protect Sydney.

"What the fuck?" I yelled. Jeff came back to the bedroom.

"How are you feeling?" Jeff asked.

"I'm in hell," I answered in earnest.

"They picked up Frank," Jeff said. "I also talked to Sydney, and she told me that you had been protecting her from her father. I don't understand why no one knew this was going on." He didn't say anything else, waiting for me to talk.

"Elizabeth told her grandfather, and I was sent here to find out if it was happening or not," I said. "Elizabeth is new to her powers, and we are still trying to keep it quiet. I couldn't understand why I was not getting better."

"Now you know. Sydney is packing two bags and then we are moving you to a safe house until you're ready to travel," Jeff said. "So, you had not been drinking human blood at the Inn?"

"God no! I was undercover to make sure Sydney lived," I said.

"Elizabeth saw her death."

"You would recover faster if you drank from one of the girls," Jeff said.

"I can't. I think I found my soul mate," I said. "I need to go home, she's there."

"When did you find her?" Jeff asked.

"She's been in my dreams. I thought she was a dream, but I found out tonight that's she real and she's in trouble." I looked over at the wall that had an imprint of my body. "I've never had a soul mate. I heard how it worked, but I didn't understand what they were talking about until now," I said. "I didn't understand the pull until now."

"The doctor is on his way over," Jeff said. "We have to find a way to get that blood out of your system before you leave."

"Uncle, are you okay?" Sydney asked, coming into the room.

"I will be," I said. "We are going to Idaho as soon as we can. I know you want to stay with Jeff's daughter, but until your dad is taken care of, you need to be in a safe place far from him." "I understand Uncle," Sydney said.

* * *

Dear Dream Lover,

I'm up after a dream I just had and its way more erotic than any others. I'm going to write how I remember them all and then how I felt after I woke up.

I close my eyes, and I hear your voice, feel your touch. I am lost in my fantasy... my nipples harden beneath my silky camisole, as heat and moisture flood my cunt. I see you rise above me, feel the weight of your body against me as you enter me, then lay on me. I can feel your arms next to me as my hands slide up your shoulders, pulling you down towards me. I shudder. I feel your breath on my neck as your lips softly graze it, searching for my own lips. I moan at the sensations, and you suckle my neck, making me moan more. As you work your way towards my lips, I am writhing beneath you, reaching out for that ultimate moment when we climax together. I feel a pulse between my legs.

As your lips reach mine, our tongues reach out and caress each other, twisting and dancing together. The taste of you arouses me all the more. As we move together, you slide all the way into me, and then slip all the way out, I moan only to have you enter me again...bringing me closer and closer to climax. I am wet, aroused, and I feel my insides quiver and pulse in excitement. I moan into our kisses; I writhe beneath you.

You slip into me yet again; this time you stay within and pump faster and harder. I feel you grow, harden and stretch me as your cock gets even bigger. I feel my walls as they stretch, burn and flood with my own juices.

I raise my hips to meet your every thrust into me, feeling my orgasm pulse and pound its way through me. I hear your moans as you reach that point, I feel your pulse, and I moan as I feel my own orgasm wash over me, drowning me in a flood of sensations. I am soaked, fully aroused, pulsing with desire and in desperate need of you. Then you bite my neck and the blood flows down my neck and over my chest. The blood didn't bug me. I find it amazing. I climax again.

I hear your moans become a shout as you explode into me, filling me with more heated pleasure and sensations. My body tingles as it feels your breath upon it. My nipples harden. You continue to thrust into me, slowing down, and eventually stopping. You lay on me and kiss my shoulder and my neck - I shudder in response, my walls convulsing around you as you pulse within me. "Call me Aramis; we are meant to be," you whisper into my ear.

My eyes pop open - my heart races, my breath is short and fast, I feel drops of sweat on my forehead and between my breasts. I grab my neck, there is no mark or blood. I lay back down to fall back to sleep.

I feel the pulses of heat and pleasure beat from within me, flooding that spot between my legs. I come to you and kiss you deeply as I wrap my arms around you. Yes, I actually flow to you. At first you just stand there, shocked at what I did. But soon enough, your arms wrap around me and you return my kiss. I feel your tongue probing my mouth, rubbing against my own. My hands are all over you one on your head, my fingers buried in your hair, the other at your neck, my nails raking across your skin. You tense at the sensation. I feel your fingers grab my hair and push my head in towards you, deepening the kiss. Your other hand is firmly on my ass, pulling me so close I can feel your arousal through your jeans.

When we finally come up for air, I push away from you. You look at me - I'm wearing a thin bra beneath my camisole and it does nothing to hide how hard my nipples are. You glance down at the rest of my attire - a short skirt, thigh-high stockings and red high heels - and as your eyes travel down, you suddenly spot my discarded thong laying on the floor. Raising your eyebrows, you look at me. I smile, walk towards you, as you begin to unfasten your jeans. I strip off your shirt and drop it to the floor. I get your jeans completely open and in one movement I pull them and your underwear down to your ankles. As your cock pops out, I get on my knees in front of you and, watching your eyes, I grab your cock with one hand, and begin to slowly lick the head. I close my eyes and moan. Smiling, I lick you oh so slowly from the bottom of the shaft, up to the head, then around it. I repeat this again and again, on the bottom, on the left, on the right - I have licked just about everywhere on your now rock hard cock. I taste your pre-cum.

I massage the shaft with one hand, and your sac with the other, still massaging and kissing the head. A few minutes later, I use my hand that's on the shaft to pull the skin of your cock down taut, towards your body, and hold it there. I kiss the tip of the head one last time. I look up at your and open my mouth and wrap my lips around the entire head, and suck your cock deeply into my mouth, until I feel the head hit the back of my throat. Pausing, I slowly back

off until I have only the head left in my mouth. I'm sucking you, keeping it "tight."

I'm still using my other hand to massage your sac, gently pinching and pulling on it as well. I keep the skin of your cock taut and suck you. I slide up and down along your cock, taking my time, ensuring I draw every ounce of pleasure into this one act.

I love to suck your cock. Just the thought of it gets me hot, wet and ready to fuck. You know this - so while I'm on my knees, eyes closed, sucking away at your cock, you bend forward and slip a hand down to grab and pinch my nipple. My eyes pop open. You put your other hand in my hair behind my neck to hold me there. I close my eyes and moan onto your cock as you pinch and pull at my nipple pulses of pleasure shoot down to my already wet pussy and explode, adding, more heat, moisture and arousal. As I moan onto your cock, I taste you drip more pre-cum, which I eagerly swallow, squeezing your cock tighter, eliciting more moans from you.

As I continue to suck you, you suddenly tell me to stop as you stop playing with my nipple. I release your cock from my mouth and look up at you questioningly. You tell me you're getting close and don't want to cum yet. I pull your pants the rest of the way off, you step out of them, and we head towards the bed. I ask what you have in mind. As we reach the bed, you pull me close and give me a full, deep, hard kiss - which I eagerly return. Backed up against the bed, you break our kiss and "push" me, so I fall back onto the bed. Getting on your knees in front of me, you push up my skirt and spread my shaved lips, exposing my pink clit and wet pussy, and proceed to lick them both.

I'm on the bed writhing and moaning as your hot, thick tongue first dips into my pussy and then slowly slides up and over my clit making me even wetter, bringing me close to orgasm. You slide one hand up to pinch my nipple - I slip my bra and camisole down for you - and use the other hand to finger my pussy as you attack my clit, licking it, nipping and even gently biting at it. Each stroke of your finger, each lick, each bite, pushes me closer and closer to the edge. Hearing my moans, seeing how turned on I am, you slip a second finger into my soaked pussy. Getting it nice and wet, you lick my clit yet again, slowly slip out both fingers and as they slide back in, one goes back into my pussy and the other in my tight ass. I gasp, wriggle and moan at the sensations that engulf my body from the inside out. You pump me, gently at first, licking my clit in time with each stroke. Then you stop licking me - you pump me faster, harder. I hear you talking to me ... "You like that? You like being fucked in both holes at once?" I moan. Again, you speak - "Yeah, you love it. You love the way it feels. You want to cum - I can feel how close you are."

I'm moaning - "Oh God - yes. Please." "Tell me," you say.

"What?" I moan.

"Beg for it. Beg me to fuck you."

"Please - Please don't stop. Please fuck me more." "Get on your knees." you say.

As I get on my knees, you stand up. You position me on the bed. "Suck my cock." I oblige, and while I'm working on your cock, I hear you get the bottle of lube off the nightstand. I hear you moan. I feel you lift my skirt, and your fingers are on me again. You slip a finger in my pussy and one in my ass and begin to fuck me. I moan onto your cock as your fingers enter me. You squeeze my pussy and ass and then relax. Your other hand is on my nipple again. I moan again. You slip your fingers out of me, and suddenly there's a loud "Slap". I jump and moan onto your cock as you spank my ass. One slap. Next you rub my ass cheeks, squeezing them. Then another slap. I moan again.

"Mmmm - You like that don't you?"

Suddenly you grab my head and force your cock all the way into my mouth as you pull your fingers out of me. I eagerly suck you. Again, short minutes go by as I suck your cock - the head hitting the back of my throat with each stroke. Your moans fill the room; the smell of sex surrounds us.

You suddenly stop and pull away, "Don't move."

I stay where I am and listen to your every move. I can tell by the sounds that you've removed the "toy bag" from its hiding place. Returning to me, you have me sit and hand me a nipple chain, telling me to put it on. I do as I'm told. I slide down the straps of the camisole and my bra. You unfasten my bra hooks and remove it. Placing the loops on my nipples and pulling them tight, my already hard nipples are even harder and are forced to stay that way. You watch and tug on the chain. I moan at the sensations that shoot from my nipples to my fully aroused pussy and ass. You slip the straps of the camisole back over my shoulders and leave the chain hanging out where you can reach it. The feel of the silk against my pinched nipples is very arousing and, closing my eyes, a soft moan escapes me.

"Since you love having both holes filled so much, we're going to have some fun," you tell me.

I see the cock you remove from the bag "It's an exact 'twin' of me," you say. You have me lay back and you use the toy in my pussy to get it wet. I am so close to orgasm - that toy hits all the right spots, and then some. You fuck me for a minute or two, then stop and pull it out. You get out the anal numbing gel and have me get on my knees so you can rub it on and in my tight ass. I moan as I feel your finger massage my tight hole, as the tingles ripple through the area when your finger enters my ass and probes it for nearly a minute.

Removing your finger, you have me turn around. Grabbing my chain, you pull me closer to you. I feel something cold on my clit. Moaning, I feel the tingles begin and I realize you've put an orgasm enhancing gel on my clit and pussy.

Oh God, I get wetter just thinking about what you're about to do to me.

You reach for the toy and slip it up into my pussy. I moan as you fuck my pussy and tug on my nipple chain.

As you're pumping me with the toy, I barely notice you slip your finger into my ass again- but once you start pumping it into me, I feel it and moan louder. The numbing gel has taken effect - as has the orgasm enhancer. I feel an orgasm building as you slip another finger into my tight ass. As it stretches open, I feel a slight burn and moan yet again.

"Yeah - you like that, I can feel how wet you are." I hear you say. "Mmm-God. Please-pant-more-gasp-make me cum, Please..." "Oh yeah - fuck my fingers baby - feel them stretch that tight ass.

You want more? Tell me."

"Yes, please, make me cum..." "No. Not yet ... you're not ready." "Yes, I am," I said.

"Please call me Aramis," you say.

I feel you stop fucking me with your fingers. Now you spread them, wiggle them, stretching my ass, making me moan more. "Oh

God. Please, Aramis..."

I woke up fast, my whole body over-sensitive, my skin especially. Every breath, every touch has me quivering. I'm weak, spent. Let's just say I have never had sex like that in real life and I'm not sure I want it. What I wanted at that moment was for you to wrap your arms around me, kiss my neck gently, and just hold me as I drift off. I did learn something from this dream though, your name is Aramis."

About the Author

Tammy Godfrey has called Southeast Idaho home for the vast majority of her life. She survived sixteen years in the military, and she is proud of almost every minute of it. After leaving the camouflage uniform behind she decided she needed to do something productive with the time that she wasn't taking care of her husband and kids. When she wasn't lost in the exciting world of tax preparation, she was hitting the books at Idaho State University seeking a degree in something practical like business. During her time in the world of academia she discovered a love for writing. After spending long days and nights overcoming her fear of the blank page her first book was published in 2013. She is currently working hard on her next novel. Tammy loves everything geek, including her adorable husband, and loves working on crafty things, reading, and going to comic con. Tammy believes that Murphy's Law has played a large part in her life. If anything, weird can happen, it will. One thing that can be said about Tammy Godfrey, she's not boring.

Milton Keynes UK
Ingram Content Group UK Ltd.
UKHW040255181024
449757UK00001B/25

9 798330 463503